WHOSE SIDE

—— *are* ——

YOU ON?

WHOSE SIDE

—— *are* ——

YOU ON?

Betty Fitzpatrick Dorion

COTEAU BOOKS
WWW.COTEAUBOOKS.COM

Edited by Bob Currie.

Cover painting by Dawn Pearcey.
Cover and book design by Duncan Campbell.
Printed and bound in Canada by AGMV Marquia.

National Library of Canada Cataloguing in Publication Data

Bertty Fitzpatrick, 1952-
Whose side are you on?

ISBN 1-55050-179-8

I. Title.
PS8557.O7473W46 2001   jC813'.54   C2001-910344-1
PZ7.D72758Wh 2001

10 9 8 7 6 5 4 3 2 1

COTEAU BOOKS
401-2206 Dewdney Ave.
Regina, Saskatchewan
Canada   S4R 1H3

AVAILABLE IN THE US FROM
General Distrubution Services
4500 Witmer Industrial Estates
Niagara Falls, NY, USA 14305-1386

The publisher gratefully acknowledges the financial assistance of the Saskatchewan Arts Board, the Canada Council for the Arts, the Government of Canada through the Book Publishing Industry Development Program (BPIDP), and the City of Regina Arts Commission, for its publishing program.

  The Canada Council for the Arts
Le Conseil des Arts du Canada 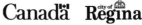 Canadä Regina

*To the young people
of St. Lawrence*

1

RON FACED INTO THE WIND, EYES SQUINTED almost shut against the brunt of the gale. Coming in off the harbour, it was wicked enough to rip the eyelashes right off your face. It probably could too. Last winter the priest lost three pairs of wiper blades driving up the shore for Sunday Mass. He said they just went perpendicular on the windshield and sailed back over the cab of his half-ton. Ron could just picture it.

He figured he wouldn't miss a few lashes but would hate to give up an eyeball. On the positive side, though, a glass eye could be a bit of fun. He'd pop it out in class to liven things up. Yeah, and Sister Carmelita would be sure to add it to her litany of nags: "Ron Tarrant, take out your book, Ron Tarrant, get those notes down, Ron Tarrant, put that eye in."

Ron scanned the road below. Blacktop, it was supposed to be. Not anymore. It was salt-bleached to a greyish white. Newer dark patches shored up the edges that were constantly eroding down the banks and into the landwash. No sidewalks, of course. St. Lawrence, though a fair-sized town by Newfoundland standards, wasn't big enough to warrant sidewalks. Besides, they probably would have crumbled just like the asphalt, eaten away by salt and washed out into Placentia Bay with the tide.

The road, officially known as Water Street, by Canada Post anyway, curved west at Riverhead Brook and wound around the bottom of the harbour. He looked over towards his house. His father came out and jumped in the pickup. Ron tensed. For no reason. Ron hadn't even seen the old man at noon; he'd been in the front room watching the news or something.

Ron jammed his hands in his pockets. His gaze followed his father's truck down the harbour. A few scattered vehicles were on the go, the bodies just as rusted as the old man's Ford. The salt again. It occurred to Ron that salt could be blamed for a lot of things here on the coast. Maybe that was the old man's problem. The salt was eating at him. Something was. Who cared? Ron was getting out as soon as he was old enough. Like his brothers. Vince and Jed worked in Toronto on construction.

Jeez. What a gale. And the clouds, low and

troublesome with enough bluster in them to bowl over a house or two in passing. Ron's clothes were being jerked and pulled as if in a brawl. At least it wasn't raining.

The road hugged the shore to the far end of town called The Dock. That's where Al lived. No sign of him. Or Bert either. Bert lived even farther – way out on the top road that ran parallel to the harbour. Ron didn't know what Canada Post called the top road. Maybe Top Street.

Usually on the way back to school, he met up with Al and Bert. He must be later than usual today.

Still, he didn't hustle. It was against his principles to hurry where school was concerned. Besides, he wanted to miss the afternoon prayer. School was penance enough, without the praying.

A quick survey of the rough grey harbour water told Ron there would be no ore boat today. Just as well. The weather was too miserable for skipping school, and Ron intended to do just that when the huge ore carrier docked.

He could see the stockpile of fluorspar against the sky further down the harbour. It had grown to forty or fifty feet in the last month or so. Around town the talk was that the miners wouldn't allow the Company to load the *Hamildoc*, now that they'd been locked out. Not until they got a contract, anyway. Could be a while. Ron shivered. Might be a bit of fun before it was all over.

A fish truck hauling a load to the plant passed below him and he got a good whiff. He yanked his collar up and turned his back to the harbour and the wind. Raw gusts raked his scalp. It was just as well he hadn't bothered combing his hair. He ran his hand over it, flattening the ripple of waves. This gale was a great straightener. Too bad it wouldn't last.

A powerful blast boosted him up the hill, but the forward list of his body wasn't entirely the wind's doing, nor the hill's. It was the bit of his father in him. The old man crossed the kitchen floor as if he were climbing the Cape. Ron didn't know he walked just like him. He would have hated it, even worse than he hated his wavy hair.

He fought the gale that blew him up Church Hill. It would take more than a good squall of wind to get him to school on time. He passed the church and then Marion Elementary. His only sister, Carrie, was in the primary wing there, grade one, and Wayne was in grade four. And they both did better than he in school.

Ron's mother lamented daily that he just didn't care. And he didn't. Once in a while he would try, but his efforts never lasted long enough to make a difference.

He turned left towards the high school, St. Augustine's, a two-storied box. Nothing to brag about. He grabbed the brass handle and yanked the door open. The wind wrenched it from his grasp and there was a resounding slam behind him. The nuns couldn't blame him this time.

He cupped his hands and blew on his stiff fingers. Sometimes this Newfoundland weather poisoned him. Here it was April, 1975, and it felt like the middle of the Ice Age.

Ron smoothed his hair. The colour of dry sand it was, and every bit as unmanageable. He pushed open the classroom door and shook his head in disgust. Bad timing. Everyone was standing for prayer and Sister Carmelita was in the middle of the sign of the cross. Now he'd have to stand there, right at the front, and pray too. He was sure he looked a sight, his wavy hair sticking out like a birch broom in fits, and his big nose as red as boiled lobster.

Sister frowned at the crucifix. It could be worse. She didn't glare at him, so he probably wouldn't have to stay after school. Not that it mattered. Just as well to be bawled out here as to be home getting heck from his old man.

Ron flicked his hand in a gesture that loosely resembled the sign of the cross. He scuffed to his seat at the back, glad that the Hail Mary had diverted attention from himself.

He pulled out a battered history book, its binding so slack the scratched-up brown cover slid around but not quite off yet. Oh well, by the time he shoved it to the back of his desk a few more times it would be off.

As Sister Carmelita tucked her broad self onto the chair behind her desk like a hen settling for a spell on a batch of eggs, Ron gauged the time. Give her four minutes, maybe five, and she'd be dozing, her head dropping in the middle of the Battle of Queenston Heights – a piece of Canadian history he'd heard enough about to remember the name, but not much more.

He leaned forward, warming to the fun about to start. Yep, there was Duck catching the eye of classmates on either side, set to line up his target, who was still droning on and on about the War of 1812. Duck flicked a few spitballs around her desk but waited till her speech slowed to a halt and her head nodded a few times and then dropped, before launching the great assault.

Ron shoved a fist to his mouth, ready to choke back a laugh, but kept his gaze on Sister's face. It was a miracle she didn't feel the stares of twenty-three pairs of eyes.

The spitball hit her square on the nose. Sister Carmelita gave a little jump, brushed at her face, and continued reading. The girls always marvelled at how she could pick up exactly where she left off. Ron never knew if she did or not; he didn't follow closely enough.

He settled back in his seat again for the endless half-hour of history which followed – a few questions, more reading. Ron knew none of the answers, but today he was lucky enough not to be called on.

Sometimes he said stupid things just to break the monotony and get a laugh. Like last week when Sister asked him on which side Tecumseh fought. He hadn't a clue. "The wrong side?" Ron had replied. Everyone tittered. Ron preened – and wound up with a detention. It had been worth it. Still, he was careful; no detentions on fine days.

Just before the afternoon break, Al, two rows over, turned around and easily caught Ron's restless eye. He raised two fingers to his lips giving Ron the "going for a smoke" signal.

The echo of the bell was still in the air as Ron grabbed his jacket from the hook in the hallway and tailed Al out the door. They streaked the twenty yards across the schoolyard to the shed, without bothering to check behind them. There was no need. While the walls of the school seemed to be all windows, the shed could be seen from none of them. It was a blind spot, about as big as the porch on Ron's house, where the boys could enjoy a peaceful smoke. As long as they remembered to get rid of the butts.

Bert and Duck were already there, huddled in the shelter of the back wall. Bert held a cigarette to his mouth while Duck tried to light it for him, both boys cupping their free hands close to the flame to cut out the draft.

The latecomers huddled in a tight circle with them till the cigarette burned red. They passed it around, stamping their feet to keep warm and dragging the hot smoke into their lungs.

Bert took a puff and handed the cigarette to Al. "The ore boat'll be in today or tomorrow," he said.

Al shook his head. He flicked the ashes. "She won't dock today, too windy."

"My old man says there's not going to be an ounce of spar loaded until the contract's signed." Duck took a long drag.

Half closing his eyes against the smoke curling in front of his face, Ron looked at Bert. "How long have they been working without a contract now anyway?" Bert should know. His father was on the union executive.

Duck cut in. "Must be two or three months."

"Closer to four," corrected Bert.

Ron passed the butt and poked his head

around the side of the shed. They couldn't hear the bell over here, but there were a couple girls still on the fire steps. "Still okay," he said, pulling back out of the wind. "Who's going to stop them from loading?"

"Mick-Joe and the boys," quipped Duck.

For half a minute Ron believed him. Mick-Joe would love it. There was a wild streak in him – and a loony one. Mick-Joe had probably already volunteered. He and his buddies were the closest thing to criminal that Ron knew. On the whole, though, it was pretty mild stuff, like selling cheap contraband cigarettes and liquor from a day trip over to St. Pierre.

Bert chuckled. "The women, that's who."

Ron looked at him. Bert must be joking. The idea of Mick-Joe was bad enough. But the women. That took the cake.

However, Bert wasn't joking. Proud of his knowledge, he parroted his father. "The men can't picket. It would jeopardize negotiations. So the women'll do it."

Ron listened with an intentness he'd never extended to any of his teachers. Somehow he couldn't picture his mother on a picket line.

"What if the boat shows up in the middle of the night?" Al asked.

"She can't," said Bert. "Dad said she's so big

she has to be guided in the harbour, in case she goes on the rocks. The best time to do it is in the daytime."

"Even if she did try to dock at night, the men on the graveyard shift would just have to make one phone call and the women'd be at the loading dock all set to picket," Duck added. "Good plan, what?"

Ron was all ears. This was the first he'd heard about the women picketing. The old man hadn't mentioned a thing. Not a word. Then again, he never said much about anything. He only opened his mouth to order someone to bring him a beer, then opened it again to guzzle it down. Unless he was bawling out Ron. A fellow didn't get much information that way.

The boys, sensing their time was up, dodged around the side of the shed, and allowed the wind to blow them back to the school.

Ron would ask the old man about the boat and the women on the picket line when he got home. He'd have to catch him in a good mood, though, or the old man would just snarl at him. He was contrary before the beer, worse when it was gone.

AFTER SCHOOL RON BROKE OFF FROM THE GANG headed down the harbour and ran up the lane to his house. He pushed open the kitchen door. Ah, there was nothing like the smell of fresh molasses buns. He reached for the plate on the table. Carrie sat at the far end, her hand propped under her chin and her pretty doll face screwed up in a pout. A half-eaten bun and two unopened story-books lay before her.

"Never mind," their mother said, "it's too miserable to go out anyway. Finish your bun and read your books." She brushed the dark curls off Carrie's face and kissed her forehead. The pout stayed.

"What's wrong?" Ron asked his little sister. He threw his jacket over the closest chair and grinned at Carrie.

"Lisa went to Bonnie's house to play and they wouldn't let me go."

Ron lifted the kettle off the back of the oil stove and, hearing water slosh around, set about making himself a cup of cocoa. "We'll fix her," he said. "The next time she comes here, we'll bar the door and won't let her in. See how she likes that."

The pout wavered. Ron could tell Carrie liked the idea. He dug into his pocket and dropped a jawteaser in front of her. She couldn't hold out. She popped the gumball into her mouth, took her books and hopped over to the daybed by the window.

Ron set his cocoa on the table. His mother slid more buns onto the plate. She rested her free hand on Ron's shoulder. The cotton print apron that stretched snug around her middle was soft on his ear. Her warmth against his skin felt good. When Dad had a few drinks in, he would say she was comfortable, a good armful.

Ron slouched lower, enjoying the heat of the oil stove on his back, and angled himself so he could put his feet on the chair at the end of the table. He was sinking his teeth into his fourth bun when Himself emerged from the front room.

Unsteady from sleep, he lurched across the linoleum floor, one hand to his head in an effort to smooth a long strand of limp grey hair over his bald spot. If he ever straightened right up, his noggin would just about graze the ceiling, Ron decided.

"A cup of tea?" said his wife, picking up the kettle.

A grunt in reply. Probably a yes, Ron figured. The old man walked past the fridge towards the bathroom. Ron could hear a harsh rattling cough, easing off, then repeated racking spasms as his father strained to clear his lungs.

His mother was standing by the stove in a world of her own. Her hand rested on the handle of the kettle as if she could hurry the boiling and get on to the next task. Absent-mindedly she tucked a curly strand of hair behind her ear. Ron got his hair from her, and Carrie got her looks.

Their mother's lips moved. Was she praying again? She was wasting her time praying for Himself. What he needed was someone to throw away his cigarettes, and it should have been done twenty years ago. The hacking cough quietened, but the worried look didn't leave his mother's face.

"Hey, Mom, are you going on the picket line?" Ron asked.

He hadn't noticed his father re-enter the kitchen. Too late to take back the words. Ron knew he was in trouble.

His father's long arm snaked out, whipped the chair away from Ron's feet. Ron scrambled to right himself. "Wha...?" he sputtered. The mug tipped. Cocoa splashed on the table and down his front. "What the...?" Ron jumped up, brushing at his sweater.

The old man yanked the chair sideways, banging it against the table leg.

Ron met his chilling glare head on. His hands curled into fists at his side. "What's your problem?" he shouted. His voice broke. Of all the times. The old man better not think he was crying. Ron choked back a swear. For his mother's sake. If it were just him and the old man, he'd curse him to hell.

His mother's voice was weary. "Leo, what do

13

you think you're doing? Can't you be civil?"

"Be civil?" her husband said. He slapped his cigarettes down. "Didn't you hear what the young whipper-snapper said?"

Slamming his fist hard on the table, so hard the plate of buns moved, he shifted back to Ron. "Like hell, she's going on the picket line. No wife of mine will set foot down there, I guarantee you that. And you stay clear too, if you knows what's good for you. The picket line – the gall."

Ron yanked his sweater over his head and glared at the stain.

His father paused. Wiped the back of his hand across his mouth. He seemed to lose some of his bluster. "They'll shut the whole place down, that's what. And then there'll be no work for anyone. Who's going to put food on the table then?

He glared at Ron. "And for bloody well sure there'll be no money for the likes of cokes and pool." He sat down hard.

"Young pups," he spat. "Get the women on the picket line. Sure. Let them do the dirty work."

Ron took the cloth from his mother and wiped up the mess on the table. Good. The old man was finally winding down. No, not quite finished yet.

"One or two years under their belts and they figures they knows it all." He took out a cigarette. His tobacco-stained finger stabbed the table.

"Twenty-six years I worked at that place. I was doing hard time there when them young pups were still in diapers. I'd just as soon shoot them as look at them, the whole lot." Disgust in every word. His father shoved the cigarette between his lips, his hand shaking in his agitation. He slapped at his pockets until he located a book of matches.

His wife set a mug of tea in front of him.

He shoved it away, tea sloshing over the rim. "Get me a beer."

Ron moved before his mother. He grabbed a beer from the fridge and the opener off the counter. He slid them onto the edge of the table. Should throw the bloody beer at him. Right now it wouldn't take much. By God, it wouldn't.

On the daybed, Carrie stared at Ron, enormous eyes peering over the top of her book.

He looked away.

2

MONDAY MORNING. AGAIN.
Ron stifled a yawn as he pushed open the classroom door. Halfway in he stopped and caught himself gawking across the room. His reaction time was never too swift in the a.m., and even worse on Mondays.

Perched on the edge of the desk was the smallest nun Ron had ever seen. She checked the clock and looked at him. Must be a substitute, though usually the subs weren't nuns. Where had they dug this one up? He eased the door shut. First impressions and all that stuff. Ron caught Al's eye and raised his eyebrows. Al winked back.

Sister hopped off the desk. Ron nodded in her general direction and strolled down the aisle to his seat.

Her voice followed him. "Good, you're here," she said. "We were waiting for you before saying prayer. The boys told me you didn't like it if we prayed without you."

Ron shook his head. They'd got him good this time. "That's right," he said. Looking as pious as he could in his semi-alert state, he extended his hands in a priestly gesture and cast his eyes heavenward. "Let's all stand."

The class burst into gales of laughter. Ron felt himself flush. Getting a laugh was a real rush. Sister had joined in, laughing as much as anybody. He wondered who she was and what she was doing here.

Then she called their attention for prayer. Instead of rattling off a regular version that they'd all learned when they were youngsters, she made it all up, or it sounded like she did, anyway.

Her eyes were closed, so it was easy to sneak a peak at her. Ron was sure she wasn't an inch over five feet. For her size, she certainly wore big glasses, enormous round lenses with black frames. They suited her though.

What had she just prayed? He thought he'd heard the word strike. Yep. He did. He knew when he saw the girls look sideways at each other as they sat down.

Strike or lockout, same thing. Company beat them to the punch and locked them out first, that's all. That riled the miners up all the more.

One thing for sure, the Company was going to pay. Yes, sir. That was all the talk these days. With the exception of Ron's house maybe. Where, if you wanted to live to eat your supper, you just didn't bring up the strike.

Sister whoever-she-was shouldn't bring it up here either.

There was an awkward quiet in the room.

Sister waited until everyone was settled before she spoke. "Now, I suppose you all want to know who I am and what I'm doing here."

Nobody said a word. But nobody fooled around either.

"Well, as I already told some of you, my name is Sister Pat. Sister Carmelita has had to go to St. John's. Her mother is seriously ill. She has cancer and is not expected to live more than a few months." She paused as if waiting for it to sink in. "So Sister has returned to St. John's to be with her. I'll be filling in, probably until June." She paced the front of the room. "I know it's late in the year for a change in teachers, but we'll have to make the best of it. I'll certainly do whatever I can to help you." She perched on the edge of the desk again.

Ron liked that. It was so normal, not like a nun at all. Then again, if Sister Carmelita had tried to sit on the edge of the desk, it would have been like shifting ballast in the hold of a cargo ship. She'd capsize for sure.

Sister Pat talked like it was a big thing, with Sister Carmelita leaving and all. There might be a way to get some mileage out of it. Nobody minded Sister Carmelita. A fellow could do lots of things in her classes, catch up on some rest, get Math homework finished, have a bit of time to himself. Yep. Sister Carm had her advantages.

Ron hoped this new Sister Pat wouldn't try to stir things up. But he was a little uneasy. That strike prayer bothered him. School was school and leave everything else out of it.

Sister held up the register. "Put up your hand when I say your name, so that I can learn who you are."

Ron shuffled to a straighter position. This could be interesting. If a few of the boys switched names, things could brighten up a bit.

But Sister Pat seemed to second-guess them. "Of course," she said, "if anyone forgets his name, we may have to meet for a half-hour or so after school and take time to get acquainted."

Ron slouched down again. So much for that. He hove up his hand as, with a slight smile, Sister called his name.

Finished, she tossed the register onto the desk. Ron had never before seen a nun toss anything anywhere. "Now," Sister said, "I have you for Religion, History, and English. We'll have to plan what we're going to do for the remainder of the year."

Marlene's hand shot up.

Ron groaned. He knew it had been too long for her to go without saying anything.

"Sister was on page 142 in our Religion book and in History she was doing the War of 1812, and transitive and intransitive verbs in English."

Bert kicked her desk from behind to shut her up, but Marlene ignored him until she was finished. Then she turned around and, with a little flick of her hand, knocked his pen to the floor. Ron grinned. He knew Bert would be cheesed off and not able to do a thing about it.

Sister Pat was still talking. "Sister Carmelita told me you haven't done any research projects yet this year."

Ernie trailed his hand lazily in the air. "She didn't do any last year either," he drawled. Ernie knew. He'd been with Sister last year.

"Well, then, it's about time we got started, isn't it?" Sister Pat's brown eyes, magnified by the glasses, penetrated the room. Ron slouched lower and ducked his head behind Donna in front of him. But he couldn't escape the perky voice. Man, he hated *perky* anytime but especially Monday mornings. "Now what are some local events, past or present, that might be interesting to research?"

Sister Pat folded her arms, leaned back on the edge of the desk, and waited. Not even the girls seemed to have any ideas. She prowled the room then, up and down rows. "What about places or buildings in town? Can you think of anything special about any of them?"

With a slight thud Ron dropped his head on his desk. This nun was going to be a pain. He knew it, just as sure as Pop Turpin knew by his arthritis that the weather was turning bad.

"Well...." said Marlene.

There she goes again. Diarrhea of the mouth.

"There's the hospital. It was built by the American government."

Sister Pat looked interested. "Now, why would the American government build a hospital in a small town on the southeast coast of Newfoundland?"

At this several of the girls put up their hands. But the good Sister chose to rouse Ernie over in the corner. "Enlighten us, Ernie."

Ernie, she called him. All the teachers called him Ernest. Ron chuckled to himself. He wasn't about to look to Ernie for enlightenment.

But, for once in his life, Ernie could answer. He leaned forward in his desk, looking quite pleased with himself. "Two American ships, the *Truxton* and the *Pollux,* ran aground at Chambers Cove and Lawn Point during the war. A bunch of sailors died. The people from the town saved whoever they could. After, the American government built the hospital to thank the town."

Al called across the room. "Good man, Ernie."

Sister ignored him. "Which war was it, Ernie?"

Ernie shook his head. "Not sure about that one. Could find out for you, though. I'll ask my dad."

Ernie was hooked. Heck, she already had him reeled in. Ron was disgusted.

"Well, Ernie, I think you might already have found your topic."

Sister turned back to the class. "Do you see what I mean? You could research some of the local businesses, find out how they came to set up in St. Lawrence."

Donna said, "But Sister, there's no books about any of that."

"You don't always need books to do research." Again she turned it back to the class. "What are some sources, other than books, that you could use?"

"Newspapers," piped Marlene again.

"That's right. Anything else?"

When nobody spoke, Sister said, "Probably the most important source you'll make use of is the interview. And she wrote it on the board in big block letters.

Ron groaned, out loud this time. Interviews, heck. They should have interviewed a bunch of different teachers instead of this one. Sister Carm was starting to look real good right now.

Prancing around at the board, her black nun garb swirling around her, Sister Pat was just getting wound up. "Let's make a list of topics that would make interesting research subjects."

Ron chuckled when Duck whispered loudly, "Billy the bootlegger. We could make a trial run to St. Pierre with him and interview his contacts."

At that Ron began to make his own list with Billy at the top. Let's see. Who else could he add? Interesting local characters worth an interview. It wouldn't be a long list, for sure. What about Mick-Joe? They could have Billy in one day to talk to the class about how he got started in the bootlegging business and then have Mick-Joe in to discuss the competition aspect.

Duck interrupted his thoughts. Duck's last name was Drake. Somebody in grade five or six called him "Duck," thinking it was good joke, and the name stuck. Duck talked all day long. But the only words the teachers ever heard him say were the ones he asked now. "Do we have to write this down?"

"Yes," Sister replied. "I'd like you to keep a

record of the topics, so that if one doesn't work out you'll have a list of the other possibilities. Of course that doesn't mean these are the only topics from which you can choose. These are just to give you ideas." She charged on. "However, if you do choose a different one, I'd like you to run it by me just to make sure you're on the right track."

She wrote "Research Topics" on the board, underlined it twice, and waited for their suggestions. When none were forthcoming, she said, writing as she spoke, "We can start with Ernie's idea. She wrote "Hospital/*Truxton/Pollux* Disaster."

Someone suggested the tidal wave of 1929. Sister added it to the list.

"Indirectly," she said, "it may have had something to do with the start-up of the mines. The cod disappeared from the area for years after the tidal wave, and so fishing was no good."

Ron had heard something about a tidal wave. A long time ago it happened. If he had to do something, this was as good as any. He'd sign up when he got around to it.

Sister went on. "Which brings us to the mines – how they got started, by whom, and what led to the present day events. Several people could work on different aspects of this topic."

The room was deathly still. No one was going to touch that one.

The bell rang for Math. Ron rooted in his desk for his book. What did this nun think she was doing? The strike was a bit of fun, something different to liven things up. But everyone knew enough to leave it out of school.

There were fellas from Salt Cove Brook in school here. The Brook boys, everyone called them. Salt Cove Brook. That's where the mines were. About three miles in off the top road. On good blacktop too. The Brook boys were bused to school every day in the Company van. They were all right, most of them, even though they were from the mainland. A few jokers tried to give them a rough time every now and then. Just because their fathers worked in the mine office and they lived in Company housing in Salt Cove Brook. Plus the fact that they got a ride to school and drove past the fellas from The Dock and top road who lived far away and had to walk no matter how dirty the weather.

There was only one girl. She was in Ron's class. Nicole. She was okay too. Well, maybe a little more than okay.

The last thing they needed here was some nun stirring things up. Why couldn't she just pray for the strikers like nuns were supposed to?

3

From the foot of the stairs, ron's mother screeched, "If you're not down here in five minutes, my son, I'm coming up."

Ron roared back. "I'm up." He waited, eyes closed.

"Yes, you're up, all right. Up in bed." Then silence.

It was a morning ritual between him and his mother. The others would have been up an hour ago. And his mother would already have called him several times; he never responded to the first few calls.

Ron was aware of his feet, cold and hanging over the end of the bed. He snagged the blanket between them and dragged it down over his toes. Better. He needed longer blankets. Man, he needed a longer bed.

Ron stretched and rubbed his eyes. What was that? He listened. There it was again. Too low for the foghorn.

He lit out of bed, wiped the moisture off the window with the lacy curtain, and peered out. The fog was still fairly thick, but there was no mistaking the ship looming in the harbour between the Cape and the Point. The *Hamildoc*. It had to be.

Ron snatched his jeans from the floor. In a frenzy he pulled them on, falling against the windowsill and scraping his arm. He swore mildly and tugged a clean sweatshirt from the pile on his chair. Everything else tumbled onto the floor.

By the time Ron finished in the bathroom, Wayne and Carrie had left for school. He downed four slices of toasted homemade bread with two mugs of tea, all the while staring intently out the window at the ship in the harbour.

His mother sighed in exasperation. "Ron, stop gaping out the window. You're going to be late again this morning." Her eyes were on the clock.

Ron knew she always kept it ten minutes ahead. "I can chew just as fast when I'm looking out the window." He drained the last of his tea. "Any more hot water?"

When he saw her look, he laughed. "Relax, Mom!"

Wiping his mouth on a dishtowel thrown on the back of a chair, he said, "I think that's the ore boat out in the harbour. Did you see it? What a cruel size!" He picked up his bag from the corner where he'd tossed it the previous night. "Guess I'll have to take a look sometime today."

His mother picked up his dishes. "Now, Ron, you make sure you goes right to school."

Ron grinned and gave her a peck on the cheek.

As he headed out the door she called after him, "I'll watch out the window and make sure you do."

He stopped at the edge of the yard and looked down the road towards the harbour, ignoring the rap on the window behind him. He couldn't see the boys. Then he heard a whistle and looked up towards the Riverhead Brook where Bert and Al beckoned him.

He sprinted till he caught up with them. "She's in, eh? That's the *Hamildoc,* isn't it?"

Bert nodded. "They got word last night that she was anchored off the Cape till morning."

All three gazed out towards the harbour. Already the fog was beginning to clear. "Sure taking a long time to guide her in," Al said.

"Well, she's a big sucker to manoeuvre. They're not taking any chances of running her aground," said Bert.

"What about the picket line?" Ron asked. "Anybody down there?"

"Anybody down there?" Bert echoed. "The

women are. Mom's been gone since three o'clock this morning. I'd love to be there myself."

"We're going down at noon. Coming?" Al asked.

"You bet," Ron replied, without a second's hesitation.

The morning dragged. By recess time the ship was at the Company dock. Nobody bothered going for a smoke. Instead, the boys hung out on the fire exit steps where they watched the harbour and commented on the size of the *Hamildoc* and what might happen. "If she ever breaks loose from there, she'll take the pier and all with her," commented Ron, eyes peeled on the harbour.

"Dad said they're underhanded enough they might try to move the ore somewhere else and pick it up there." That was Bert with his inside information.

"Not a chance." Al shook his head. "The women'll be watching every move they make."

Duck nodded. "That's for sure. They're not letting one truckload of that ore go anywhere."

After recess there was Math and then Perky Pat. Ron was pleased with himself for having come up with the nickname. No one called Sister Pat that to her face, but even the girls admitted that it fit.

"If you haven't chosen a subject for your

research report yet, think about it fast." That was how she started class. "I want your topic by the end of the day or you'll have to meet with me after school to choose one."

Ron sighed and waved his hand at Perky.

"Yes, Ron?"

"I'll probably do the tidal wave."

"Sorry, Ron, it's already taken." She didn't sound the least bit sorry. "You'll have to pick something else, I'm afraid."

Perky was no help for sure. Irritated, Ron said, "I could do a different aspect of the tidal wave, y'know, like you want for the strike. I could do the point of view of the fish that were never seen again." There were titters. "Or those washed out to sea."

Sister Pat cut him off. "Are you finished, Ron? Some of the people who lost family in that disaster, or who lost homes and all their possessions, might not find your flippant attitude so amusing."

The room was quiet. "I guess so," Ron muttered, knowing his face was red. He didn't know what had made him say that. All he knew was he felt like bugging her. But he didn't feel any satisfaction. To heck with it all. He'd do what he always did, as little as possible. The maddening thing was he had a feeling that Perky Pat wouldn't be satisfied with that. It would be too bad if, with a few months of school left, she made him fail. Just because he didn't work his butt off on her perky little assignments. Too bad Sister Carmelita had to leave.

At noon Ron walked out of class without giving Perky a topic. He'd slip something on her desk before the day was over. One thing for sure. He wasn't staying after school for a "talk."

He grabbed his jacket from the hook and fell in with Bert and Al. On the way past his house, he walked on the far side of the boys, away from the house. No sign of Wayne or Carrie. He'd deal with the questions from his mother when he had to.

If there was ever a good day for being on a picket line, this was it. The fog had cleared off completely. The sun was shining and the breeze was beautiful, gentle and warm. Ron pulled off his jacket and tossed it on the fence post by Paddy's garage. He'd pick it up on his way up the harbour.

As they approached the dock, he could see a crowd of women near the ramp the trucks used to dump the ore. They were standing around in small groups talking and laughing. Below the ramp, another group stood by the gates in front of a mountain of spar. Those gates would have to be opened in order to load the spar onto the *Hamildoc*.

Three or four women sat on the grass singing from a song sheet and another on a rock behind them played the guitar. A case of soft drinks and tins of cookies and sandwiches lay on the grass.

"Where's Mom?" Bert asked Al's old lady.

"She went home about an hour ago to get a bit of rest. She was here all night," Mrs. Edwards told him. "I wants you to go home and get your brother his lunch," she ordered Al. "Open a can of spaghetti for him. And don't forget to clean up your mess."

"Can't I stay here?" Al asked. "We can run and get coffee and stuff. Right, Ron?"

"The best way you boys can help is by going to school and not having us worry about what you're up to. Now grab a sandwich and a drink and get along."

Ron held the sandwich bag between his teeth and caught the cupcake Al tossed him. Food in hand, the three headed down the bank for a closer look at the *Hamildoc*.

Mrs. Edwards called after them. "Get out of there now."

Al called back. "Yeah, we're just having a look before we go."

From where they stood on the waterfront, the

ore carrier was enormous. Its massive hull had more rust than black paint on it. And the top was a dingy yellowed-white. They sure hadn't dressed her up to come to town.

"Looks like they're not big on swabbing decks," Al said.

"Must be just in the movies they do that," Ron replied.

There wasn't a sign of life aboard.

"They're sure keeping out of sight," Bert commented.

"Probably afraid of the women," Al scoffed.

"Most likely they're under orders to lay low." This from Bert. Bert overdid it sometimes, with his dad being head of the Union. Ron thought he was probably right this time though.

"Well, I think I'll head home," Bert announced, through a bite of sandwich. "Dad had a Union meeting this morning. Maybe he'll have some news."

Al took aim and smashed his empty Coke bottle against a sizable rock in the landwash. "Not much action here yet." He turned back towards the road. "Catchya later, Ron."

"Yeah," Bert added. "I'll let you know if there's anything new."

"Sure." Ron picked up a rock and hucked it towards the ore boat. Didn't even come close. The next try he took more careful aim. Better, but it plopped in the water nowhere near close enough to even make a splash on the bow.

Ron strolled along the shore. Bert was lucky having his father in the Union. And with his mother on the picket line, he was right in the middle of everything. Al too. Some guys had all the luck. He kicked at a jellyfish blob.

With the tide out, the strand, imprinted with wave lines, was hard-packed. Hardly left a footprint. His old man, too miserable to talk to, probably wouldn't even take part in the strike. Ron hoped to God he would at least go on the picket line when it was his shift.

He turned up his nose at the stink of rotting fish and hopped over two dead sculpins.

What if the old man refused to help? Wouldn't even go on the picket line? The boys would razz him about it for sure. And what would he say? What could he say?

He picked his way around a slab of slimy rock, knowing from experience how slick it was. When he came to Dudler's tiny shop, out in the landwash like some *National Geographic* picture of them houses stuck up on stilts somewhere in the Pacific, he climbed the bank and walked up the harbour again.

He picked his jacket off the post. As he turned

up the lane, Carrie ran towards him on her way back to school. "Where were you?" she asked, her black eyes solemn.

He lifted her off the ground and swung her around until she squealed with delight. Setting her down, he hung onto her until he was sure she was steady on her feet. She looked up at him. "Dad's some mad at you," she said, her tiny forehead creased in a frown.

Ron pretended to be horrified. "I'm afraid. Can you come in with me?" He grabbed her small hand and pulled her towards the house.

She liked that. She giggled and pulled free. "You're crazy, Ron," she yelled as she ran off.

Ron wiped the grin off his mug and tightened his gut before going in to face the music.

His father sat at the end of the table. He glowered at Ron and forked some chicken hearts into his mouth. It seemed to Ron his mother was always slow-cooking chicken hearts for the old man. He had them at least three or four times a week. Suited him to a tee. Chicken-hearted was what he was.

He tore apart a slice of bread and growled at Ron. "Where were you? You should've been home here a half-hour ago."

Ron thought, what's it to you?

The old man wiped his chin with his hand.

"Were you down at that ore boat? I told you if you went near that place...."

Ron raised his voice. "I wasn't down there."

"You weren't down there," his father snorted. "Then where were you all this time? Answer me that."

"Look, I said I wasn't." The old man couldn't prove anything.

Mom stood at the stove. She knew. "Now Ron, be civil. Sit down and have a bite to eat before you goes back to school."

"Yes," his father cut in, "you better grub up now while there's still something in the cupboard." Neither Ron nor his mother made any attempt to stop him from getting wound up. "We'll see how you feels about the 'strike' when there's nare bit in the house to eat." He glared at Ron. "When you're good and hungry."

Ron jumped up. "Lost my appetite," he said, and left in a huff.

He felt sorry for his mother, stuck in the house with Him.

Too early to go to school yet. If he went. He kicked a loose piece of asphalt by the side of the road and sent it flying. With the toe of his sneaker, he broke off another. If he stayed here, his mother'd be rapping at the window any second. He might as well dodge across the causeway to Gus's.

The place wasn't Gus's anymore though. He'd gotten sick with the miner's disease and died last year. But everyone still called the little shop at the end of the causeway Gus's. Now it was owned by some fellow from Lawn. You could buy cigarettes, loose. No one asked any questions.

Ron didn't bother with the steps. He was about to hop up from the other side when he heard his name. Walking along the shore road was Nicole. She waved.

He stayed where he was and waited for her. His hand shot to his head to smooth his hair. Why hadn't he at least looked in the mirror before leaving the house?

"Hi there," Nicole called.

Ron hoped his deodorant was working. Couldn't smell anything. He jumped back from the step and walked to meet her.

"What are you doing here?" she asked. "Don't you live over by the soccer field?"

She knew where he lived. He didn't miss a beat. "What about you? What are you doing around the shore?"

"I went to eat lunch with Margie. She sprained her ankle yesterday playing softball."

Ron hadn't noticed Marg wasn't at school. But he nodded, as if some great mystery had just been cleared up. There was an awkward silence. He didn't have a clue what to say next, that is, until he heard himself spout, "Well, we're going to be late for school if we don't get moving."

Of all the dumb, stupid things to say. As if he, Ron Tarrant, ever cared about being late for school.

Nicole wrinkled her nose at him. "Let's go then. I don't want to be blamed for making you late."

Ron grinned and fell into step with her. He knew his face was flushed, and he was grinning like an idiot. The breeze blew her long brown hair close to his shoulder. Nice.

"Isn't this a gorgeous day?" she said. "On the prairies where I used to live, we had lots of beautiful weather like this, sun every day."

"We do too," Ron said. "It's just that the clouds covers it up for weeks at a time. That way we appreciates these fine days when we gets them – every six weeks or so."

She wrinkled her little nose again and laughed up at him. Ron wanted to make her laugh every time he opened his mouth.

They walked up Church Hill.

"Who do we have first?" Nicole asked.

Ron shrugged. "Does it matter? They're teachers. They're all the same."

"No, they're not," she argued, giving him a playful shove.

Inside, Nicole spotted Sister Pat in the hallway and called out to her. "Sister, I checked with Margie at noon and we're going to work together on the report."

"Oh, yes." Sister whipped a black notepad out of the folds of her garb. "What was it again?"

"The history of mining in St. Lawrence. From the time the mines first started...."

Sister looked up from her notepad. "Including the strike?"

"No, not the strike. My dad said it would be better if I didn't do that."

Sister nodded. "The strike would be heavy, along with the history." She looked at Ron. "What about you, Ron? Have you decided?"

"I'll do it," he said.

"Which topic?" Sister asked.

"The strike."

Perky wrote it in her book. Too late. There it was. Straight from his mouth, no input from the brain at all.

"Have you thought about which aspect you'd like to tackle?"

He hadn't. He didn't know what she was talking about. "Uh, no, uh...."

She smiled brightly at him. "Never mind. Think about it and I'll talk to you later in the week."

Ron sauntered into class and sat down. The

bell hadn't even rung. He pressed the dull lead of his pencil into the old wooden desktop, marking the word STRIKE in heavy dark strokes. Then he traced the letters over and over again, until they sank into the grain of the wood. There. Try to wash that off.

What aspect would he tackle? He was going to tackle his old man. And bring him down.

When his father saw strike clippings and stuff lying around, he'd flip his lid.

Ron couldn't wait to get started.

4

RON SPRINTED OVER THE ROAD AS FAR AS THE causeway. Man, Friday evenings made life worth living. He was heading down the harbour to Harry's hangout. Better slow down. He'd just plastered his hair into place with the aid of a gallon of water. No sense in letting his efforts go to waste. Reaching into his pocket, Ron felt the dollar bill his mom had poked in his hand before he left the house.

He flung his arms out to let the breeze get at his pits. Would Nicole be there tonight? Maybe he'd get up enough nerve to ask her to play a game of pool, or go for a walk or something. His insides did a little flip at the thought and a grin took over his face.

When Ron got to Harry's, he had to wait to get in. The doorway was crowded, one gang going in and another leaving and all yakking in the entrance. Ron wiped his sweaty palms on his jeans. He edged inside. A quick scan of the dim room. No sign of her. He let out an uneven breath, part disappointment, part relief.

There was Al draped over the jukebox. Ron lit out across the floor, reached around him and pressed C-11 before Al knew what was happening.

Al swung around and swore. "What do you think you're doing, Tarrant?" He moved to grab Ron around the neck. "You owe me a quarter, buddy."

Ron skidded out of Al's way. He had no intention of getting caught in Al's powerful clutches. He laughed when The Jackson Five started singing "Kansas City." "Thanks for playing my song, Al." When Al came for him again, Ron said, "C'mon, I'll beat you at a game of pool."

While Ron racked up the balls, Al grabbed a pool cue and started playing a mean guitar with it. Then, the jukebox incident already forgotten, he sang at the top of his lungs. And Al had good lungs. "...I'm goin' to St. Lawrence City, St. Lawrence City here I come...."

Most ignored him. One of the girls yelled across the room, "Yeah, Al!"

Ron grinned and shook his head. Al was crazy, always had been. Ron broke the balls and pocketed the seven and the one before he missed.

Al liked to call the game as he was doing now.

In a hushed tone he announced, "Four ball, side pocket."

"Shut up," Ron said. Al might be crazier, but Ron was a better pool player. Minutes later Ron sent the eight ball down to the corner pocket, ending the game. "Loser pays for the next one," he said.

"And who's the loser?" asked a voice behind Ron.

Ron turned around. There was Nicole, Coke in hand, smiling at him. She must have walked right past him to get to the machine. And he hadn't even seen her. Grinning, he thumbed at Al who was putting a quarter in the slot.

"I didn't win, but I ain't no loser," Al wailed in a thick country twang.

Ron ignored him. "I didn't see you come in," he said.

Nicole was still laughing at Al's silliness. "I know," she said. "I was watching you play. You're pretty good."

Ron's heart soared. About to lay a hand on her shoulder, he stopped in mid-air and scratched his head – not too much, didn't want to mess up the mop. He grinned at her. "I have to agree with you." For Al's benefit he added, "Of course, it helps when the competition's not that great."

She laughed. "No conceit in your family; you have it all."

Ron laughed with her.

Al noisily racked up the balls. "Well, let's go, hot shot!"

Nicole smiled straight at Ron. "See you later."

"You bet," Ron replied, softly so Al wouldn't hear.

He was sure she blushed as she walked away. Had he done that? He'd never made a girl blush before.

In a daze Ron turned towards the pool table. Al let out a low whistle. "Now that's some cute," he said. "You hit the jackpot, buddy."

Ron chalked his cuestick. Mr. Cool. Except he couldn't stop grinning.

Al broke and pocketed a four, a six, and then a two before the cue slipped and Ron got a turn.

Ron missed on the first shot. His eyes kept straying across the room. Al beat him easy.

"Why don't you go talk to her?" Al asked. They perched on stools at the counter.

"I dunno. Maybe. Who's she with?"

"There's a bunch of them. Her sister is there."

Ron nodded. He hated to go over there with her older sister around. But he didn't want to miss this chance either. He eased his lean frame off the stool and took his time looking around the room. There she was.

Nicole brushed her hair off her face and wiggled her fingers at Ron in a tentative wave.

He ambled across the room. She looked his way. He hesitated midway and jerked his head towards the door. What if she said no? Or ignored him? Man, this was tough.

Nicole nodded briefly at Ron and spoke to her sister. The sister looked at her watch and said something. Nicole walked towards Ron. Smiling.

Ron began breathing again, in fits and starts.

He was aware of nosy looks as they walked out the door. One of the grade eight fellas, on his way in, looked at Nicole and said, "All right, Ron, way to go."

Ron punched his shoulder.

The fog had settled closer, in their faces. And the mist was close to rain. Nicole zipped up her leather jacket. It was real leather too. You could tell by the way it was worn soft and not all cracked. With a jacket like that, she must be rich.

They walked up the harbour, away from the women on the picket line. Breathing was easier out here.

"I can't stay long," Nicole said. "We have to have the car back by ten. My dad has to go on night shift."

"How come your old man has to work nights? I thought everything was shut down."

"He's management. So he has to keep an eye

on things. Just in case something happens."

Ron picked up a rock and tossed it with considerable force into the landwash. He tried to keep the edge out of his voice. "What does the Company think the miners are up to? Trying to sabotage the place?"

Nah, she wouldn't think that.

Nicole shrugged and jammed her hands in her pockets.

"Not likely." Ron couldn't leave it alone. "They do want to go back to work when this is all over."

"I know that," she said.

There. She hadn't meant anything by it. Just an innocent comment. They had walked as far as the wharf. Ron steered her towards it, but Nicole stopped walking. "I'd better not," she said. "Alli told me to stay in sight so she can find me."

"Fine. I'll go by myself," Ron joked.

She laughed and sat on the steel guardrail that edged the road above the landwash. "Let's sit here."

He perched next to her. Across the road the light-pole lamp flicked on. The light was useless, drained away in mid-air by the fog.

Ron took Nicole's hand.

She stretched her palm along his.

Before he even had a chance to savour how

46

good her hand felt, Mick-Joe and his gang of idiots passed, hooting and swearing at anyone in sight.

Ron felt Nicole stiffen. "They won't hurt you," he reassured her.

"Hey, Tarrant," one of Mick-Joe's goon friends called out. "Suckin up to the Company, eh?"

Then Mick-Joe. "Yeah, like his old man." A string of foul language followed.

"What's he talking about?" Nicole asked.

"Nothing," Ron replied. "They're imbeciles. Ignore them." He grinned at her. "They're only allowed out of the cage at night."

Nicole laughed, but it had a nervous edge.

A car horn blew then and a Ford station wagon stopped on the road. "I have to go," she said.

Ron nodded and watched her leave. "See you."

She waved from the back seat. He waved back. He didn't even feel silly. Only out of sorts.

He gave the guardrail a vicious shove with the sole of his sneaker. What rotten luck for Mick-Joe to come along when he did. Saying Ron was like his old man. There was no way he was like his old man. No way. Absolutely.

Ron didn't go back to the hangout. Just didn't feel like it. Instead, he scuffed home, kicking rocks out of his way with a vengeance.

"You didn't stay long," said his mother when he pushed open the door.

"Girlfriend must've dropped him," quipped Wayne, steering out of Ron's reach on his way to the front room with a fistful of jam-jams.

Ron glared at him. "Shut up, brain." Wayne hated to be needled about his smarts. Too bad. He shouldn't be acting so smart-mouthed.

Ron strolled into the living room where his brother joined Carrie, who was watching a Columbo movie on TV. Ron tried to turn the channel to baseball, but they put up such a squall he had to change it back.

Usually he could buy Wayne off with a tomorrow promise to kick the ball around the front yard. Not this time. Wayne must be really ticked off about the "brain" crack.

Ron grabbed him from behind and they started to wrestle. Little brother was getting stronger. Carrie turned the volume on the television up full blast and roared over the noise, "I'm telling Mom."

"All right, you little tattle-tale," Ron said, and dumped his brother in a heap on the chesterfield.

Back in the kitchen he hunted in the cupboard for something good to eat, but couldn't find anything. The phone rang and he picked it up. "Mom, where's Dad?"

"At the Stella Maris."

"He's at the club." Bert's dad was on the other end.

Ron replaced the receiver and told his mother, "That was Sid Slaney. He said to ask Dad if he'd be able to go on tonight at twelve instead of tomorrow."

His mother nodded.

"Go on what?" Ron asked.

"On his shift...on the picket."

"I didn't think he was going to go. That's what he said."

"Don't mind your father. He says lots of things."

Ron raised his eyebrows. The old man must be coming around then. Well, that was something.

Nicole had said her old man had to work tonight. They'd be in there together. Ron wondered if they'd be anywhere near each other, if they even knew each other. Not likely. With her old man being in management and all. What if his father did or said something and Nicole's father talked about it at home? God, he hoped not.

The door opened then and in he came. Ron glanced at him to gauge his mood. Not too bad by the looks of him. "Hey, Dad," he said, in greeting.

His father grunted something back, a fairly

49

pleasant grunt though, Ron thought.

Then Ron's mother mentioned the phone call and the old man's mood changed as sudden as that. He let out a string of swear words that impressed Ron, who thought he knew a few good ones. But he had to hand it to the old man. Some of these were original.

His wife tried to hush him. "For God's sake, Leo, watch your mouth. The children can hear you in the next room."

Ron noticed she didn't include him with the children. He was starting to get some respect around here. About time.

The old man quieted down a bit then. Ron was amazed that sometimes his dad actually seemed to listen to Mom. Whether he really did or not, Ron didn't know, but sometimes when Mom got after him it looked like he was ashamed of the way he'd carried on.

In Ron's eyes his mother was a saint, the way she put up with the old man, tolerating his tantrums and his drinking. As far as Ron was concerned she didn't set him straight often enough.

Seeing her now, looking so drained as she sat by the stove, Ron decided to try and smooth the old man's feathers, for her sake.

"Where's my work clothes?" his father muttered.

"Hanging in the porch where they always are."

She moved to get up.

"I'll get them," Ron said. "Why do you need work clothes anyway? You won't be doing anything in there. Will you?"

His father sat down at the end of the table. "And what makes you think you knows so much?"

Ron shrugged, determined to remain pleasant. "Do you know a fellow named Kosheluk who works in there?"

His father pulled on a grey wool sock. "I don't want to know him. He's slack-ass management."

Ron grinned at his dad's assessment of Nicole's father. Guess they wouldn't be friends. "Yeah, Dad," he said. "You're starting to talk like a striker."

Bad choice of words. The old man went berserk. Ron hadn't meant to push his button, but wasted no time in putting some distance between himself and the old man.

He jumped to his feet, waving his fist at Ron, the other wool sock flopping around in front of his face. "Striker." He was livid. "Is that all you have on your brain these days? Let me tell you something. What I thinks of management is what I always thought of the scum. And I thinks the same thing of the bloody young pups who started this whole thing. They're even bigger scum."

He yanked open the kitchen door and left, leaving it and the porch door swinging behind him.

Ron closed them both. The sound of the truck roaring out of the yard filled the kitchen.

His mother sighed. "Ron, will you phone Sid Slaney and tell him Dad left to go work the shift?"

As he hung up, the movie ended, if the noise from the front room was anything to judge by. Wayne and Carrie piled out for a lunch before bed.

"Mom," Ron said, "I need to buy a paper tomorrow."

"What for?" cracked Wayne. "You can't read."

Ron clipped him in the side of the head. Wayne came back with a hip check before making his escape.

Ron's mother asked, "What do you need the paper for?"

"School. Got to do some research." There. That would put a smile on her face.

It didn't quite.

He wouldn't mention what he wanted to research. Not tonight.

5

"S t. Lawrence Dispute...."

"New Contract Won't Settle Real Issues"

Those were the headlines in the *Evening Telegram*. Of course, it wasn't front page or anything, page five actually. Not too often a small town like St. Lawrence took up a whole page in the St. John's paper.

Ron leaned closer. He knew all the fellows in the picture, Mike Fitzpatrick, Terrence Slaney (that was Tay), Lance Slaney (they got his name wrong, it was really Lon), and the union president, Bert's dad. With a mountain of spar in the background.

He checked out the articles, grinning at the one on the bottom, "Women Not Afraid of Company." The article started by quoting words from a song one of the women, Tess Barry, had made up.

We're the wives of the miners.

We're fed up to the chin.
We're doin what we can
to show support for our men.
They gave us no choice
when they locked up the mine.
We'll stay while we're needed on the picket line.

Ron chuckled. Good for Tess.

He read on. "'All we can do is sit and watch the men perish,' Tess said. A mother of four" – Ron wondered who it was – "added, 'What's going on here affects all of us. One of us might be the next one to join the two hundred or so widows in this community.'"

Ron knew there were lots of men who had died of the miner's disease. He could name quite a few himself if he put his mind to it. And those were just relatives of schoolmates. Then there were others he'd heard Mom or Dad say had to come off work, or had to go to St. John's for treatment. But almost two hundred? Sure, there were only about two thousand people in the whole place.

"Hey, Mom, the paper said that close to two hundred men here died from the miner's disease."

She wiped a dish and put it in the cupboard. "God rest their souls."

"Who are they all?"

"Now Ron, that's since the mines opened in the thirties, you know. But sure, there's been five in the last year alone. There's poor Benny Clarke, Ves Pike, Rick Slaney.... Then there's Herb Fitzpatrick, and Rudy Turpin, only forty-one years old. There's something wrong somewhere when young men like that start dying."

Ron figured this was as good a time as any to tell her about the report. "That's what my research is about. The mines — and the strike. That new nun I was telling you about, Perky Pat, she's making us do it."

His mother shook her head. "Now don't you be disrespectful," she said.

She seemed more ticked off about his lack of respect than she was about his doing his report on the strike. Oh, well. At least she was more reasonable than the old man.

"And don't you throw that strike business in your father's face. You know how he feels about it."

"How come he's so against it? He'd make more money, wouldn't he?"

"Well, there's more than money, Ron."

"Like what?"

She sighed and shook her head.

"Like what?" he asked again.

"Like what if they shuts down the Company altogether and there's no jobs at all? Your father is too old now to pick up and move somewhere else and start over. He's got a houseful of young ones to look after. It's fine for you to talk."

"Aw, they'll never move out of here. They're making too much money. Bert's dad said."

"Bert's dad don't know everything."

"At least he's trying to do something. Not like Dad."

There was silence.

Ron folded the newspaper and threw it across the kitchen to the daybed, where it lay with page five up. Good. He rose, pushing the table back with a loud scrape.

"Ron, don't be so rough."

"Perky wants us to interview people. For that report. Who do you think I could talk to?"

"Probably the best person would be Mr. Bennie Lake. He was with the mines a long time."

"Does he still work there?"

"No, Ron, Mr. Bennie's old now, he's retired. I don't think he's too well these days though."

"Where does he live?"

"In The Bottom, with his daughter. His wife died a couple years ago and he moved in with Rita. You know, the Haskells. The girl is in your class."

"Jackie. Do you think he'd mind talking to me?"

"You won't know till you ask."

"Jeez, I wish that nun would go back where she came from. This is all a bunch of garbage. Who cares what some old geezer has to say? I know I don't. I'm out of here as soon as I'm old enough. Yes, sir. The day I turn sixteen, I'm gone."

"Is that right?"

What kind of an answer was that? Ron was browned off, with her, with everything. "What do you care anyway?" He picked up the paring knife from the counter and stabbed the loaf of bread.

She took it from him and dropped it in the sink.

"Will you phone him for me?"

"Me? Sure, 'tis not my paper."

"Aw, c'mon Mom," he coaxed. "You know him. I don't."

His mother dried her hands on her apron. "You may as well give up, Ron. You could be in The Bottom and back in the time you waste nagging me."

Nagging. He didn't nag. Only old people nagged. Like nuns. And some mothers.

God, he hated school. Especially Perky and her stupid *perky* ideas. He grabbed a knife from the drawer, hacked off a slice of bread and slapped on bakeapple jam. Tomorrow was the soccer game against Grand Bank and he wasn't missing that.

Damn. He supposed he'd have to do it today.

Might as well get it over with.

In the yard, Wayne wanted to know where Ron was going.

"None of your business." Ron weaseled the ball from him and slogged it at the fence.

"You said you'd have a game tomorrow."

"Yeah, tomorrow."

"It's tomorrow now."

"What school do you go to, my son? It's today."

Wayne planted his hand on his bony little hip and looked up at Ron. "No, you said yester-day...."

"Right, tomorrow."

"Arrhhh," Wayne charged at him, but Ron laughed like a maniac and hopped the fence, leaving Wayne standing there, fists up.

He sobered once he left Wayne behind. What kind of a fool was he, doing this? He'd rather – he didn't know what he'd rather be doing – anything instead of this. Be seasick for a week. Clean ten dozen squid. Lick the rust off that ore carrier. Anything.

He looked up to see Mick-Joe and his buddy, Lar, coming around the Riverhead bend. The last person Ron needed to see right now was Mick-Joe.

Mick-Joe veered towards him with Lar in tow.

He stopped on the road and saluted a Mountie cruiser going by. But the Mountie pulled over and got out.

Ron used the opportunity to get away. He took the shortcut. Sauntered across the field as if he didn't have a care in the world. If Mick-Joe was watching, Ron didn't want to be seen running.

But no matter how slow he walked, every step took him closer to the ranch-style fence around the small green bungalow with the veranda and the white door.

He knocked. Softly. Maybe there was nobody home.

Jackie opened the door. She didn't say a word, just looked up at him, and slid her finger along her nose to push up her glasses. He could have been a post on the veranda for all the interest she showed.

"Uh...hi, Jackie."

"Hi."

He always said hi to her in school and she always said hi back. That was all, and it looked like it was all now too.

"I came to see your grandfather...uh, about the report...uh, we have to do...the strike."

She smiled. No, it was more than a smile. She was laughing, not out loud, but she was definitely laughing. And her cheeks were getting pinker.

So were Ron's. He didn't know what was so funny.

"You want to see Grandad?" She bit her lip.

"Yeah. What's so funny?"

"You! This is the wrong place if you want the Company's side. Grandad is a Union man!"

"What makes you think I want the Company side?"

"You seem pretty cosy with the Company to me." She was laughing at him again.

He knew she was talking about Nicole. And his face was painfully red. "What's it to you?" he muttered.

Jackie was serious now. "Well, you better decide. Grandad isn't feeling that good and you better not be wasting his time."

"If that's the way you feel, I'll leave." Ron stepped back, stumbled, and missed the top step. He grabbed the railing and swore, not quite under his breath. Jackie sure had a lot more to say at home than she did at school.

A man peered out from behind Jackie. Ron recognized him. Her grandfather looked like he was wasting away. The colour of death, his mother would say.

"Well, who's this?" He looked from Jackie to Ron and winked. "No visiting with young fellers on the veranda now."

Ron had to laugh. Jackie didn't know what to say. She looked like she wished the floor would swallow her up. Ron loved it. He laughed with her grandfather and said, "I'm Ron Tarrant."

Mr. Bennie Lake nodded. "Are you Leo's boy?"

"Yes, sir."

"You look more like your mother. Got Leo's height though."

Too bad. Wasn't Ron's choice.

"If you don't mind, Mr. Lake –"

"Call me Bennie, son. Or I mightn't know who you're talking about. Bennie's the name."

"Okay, sir. Mr. Bennie. Uh...uh...I'd like to talk to you about the mines and the strike. I got this report to do for school."

Mr. Bennie nodded. "Come in, come in. Must be the same one Jackie has. You in the same class?"

Ron nodded.

Jackie seemed to have run out of words.

He followed Mr. Bennie into the large kitchen, where the older man eased himself into an armchair by the window and motioned to Ron to sit down across from him. Jackie stood by the counter. Ron didn't look at her.

"You know, that's a smart thing that little nun is doing."

Jackie cut in. "Ron doesn't think so. He made

up a name for her. Perky Pat."

Man, he could have jabbed her one. What had he ever done to her? Ron could only look down at his feet and take it.

Mr. Bennie sipped from a mug. He took his time about it. Then he set the mug on the windowsill and laughed, a raspy sound. "Perky Pat, that's not so bad. I've heard worse in my day."

Ron raised his head and grinned. Hey, the old man was all right. Too bad he couldn't say the same for the granddaughter.

Mr. Bennie leaned back in his chair. "This is what I'll do," he said, staring out the window. "I'll tell you about the mines, you and Jackie, if that's what you wants. But I'll talk to you both at the same time and you can pick what you like out of it." He looked at Ron. "There's one more thing. When your paper is done, I'd like a copy." He leaned forward. "Is that a deal?"

A slight nod from Ron. Ever so slight. He felt like he was signing his life away. He'd have to do a good job, whether he wanted to or not. This was getting to be too serious. Made him nervous.

Jackie nodded at her grandad too.

A good job shouldn't be too much trouble for the brain here. She probably never got a mark under ninety-five in her life. Come to think of it, he didn't know what her marks were. She wasn't one to broadcast them, like Marlene and a few others. He knew she did good from the way the other girls talked. He never knew she had such a mouth.

Now seemed like a good time to leave. Ron stood up.

"Uh, what time...when would we be able to start?"

"How about Monday?" Mr. Bennie said. "After supper?"

Ron nodded. He wondered if he had anything going on Monday evening. He couldn't think.

Jackie glowered at him as he brushed past. She pushed her glasses up on her nose. He'd bring her some Crazy Glue Monday evening. If he remembered. If he showed up.

"What's the matter?" he muttered. "Afraid you might have to share a bit of information?"

"Just don't pass it on to your Company friends," she said quietly.

In his hurry to leave, Ron almost bumped into Mrs. Haskell in the doorway. At the surprised look on her face, he felt the red come on. "Sorry," he mumbled, and hurtled down the three steps.

He took the shortcut home. His mind was a jumble. He looked across the road towards the graveyard. Lots of miners there, one of them an uncle of his.

He remembered when Uncle Phil died, just

barely. It must have been seven or eight years ago. All he could recall was how uncomfortable he'd felt seeing the ghost of his uncle lying in the bed, so thin Ron wouldn't have recognized him, and the women standing around in the bedroom like the holy picture that hung in his parents' bedroom, the one of Joseph dying in the arms of Jesus and Mary. All he'd wanted to do was get out of there fast.

He took off running now. This stupid strike paper was not one of his brightest ideas. He didn't need this. He swore as water seeped into his runners. This part of the field was nothing but a bloody bog.

Ron's eyes were drawn to the harbour. The newspaper was right: the graveyard on one end of town and at the other end a huge pile of spar, the houses in between, caught between the two. Some choice.

He breezed into the kitchen to hear his father coughing his innards up in the bathroom. By the rattling sound, his rib cage must have worked itself loose and was coming too.

Carrie attached herself to Ron's waist and stepped on his feet, demanding to be walked across the kitchen. He obliged her and then turned her upside down and deposited her, shrieking with delight, on the daybed.

"Watch her neck, Ron," warned their mother,

on her way upstairs with a load of clean clothes.

When he turned, Carrie, still shrieking, jumped on his back. Ron, bending to hoist her higher, saw it coming but not in time to stop it. The rolled up newspaper whacked Carrie's behind.

Their father barked. "Stop that horsing around, or I'll give you something to screech about."

Carrie's squeals turned to sobs. Ron pulled her around so she sat on his hip. She buried her face in his neck. "What'd you do that for?" he snapped at his father. "It eats you up to see anyone having a bit of fun."

His father snapped back. "Listen to your mother when she's talking to you." Scowling at Ron, Carrie, and everything else, he hauled out the chair as if he was mad at that too. He sat down and smoothed out the paper, still open on page five.

Ron waited. This should be good.

The old man grunted when he read the headline.

Ron couldn't resist. "Don't throw it out when you're finished with it," he said.

No response.

"I need it to do a report for school. On the strike."

A snort.

"Well, there's more where that one came from anyway."

Ron lowered Carrie, still whimpering in his arms, to the floor.

His father looked up then. "Carrie, bring me a beer."

He laid a nickel on the table.

Instantly over her hurt feelings and sore behind, Carrie ran to the fridge. Well trained, she returned with the beer and an opener.

She wrestled with her father's finger until she was able to grab the trapped nickel. "I'm going over to Bill's," she announced, "to get some bubble gum."

"Watch the cars," her father said, going back to the paper.

Ron hung around.

The old man muttered, swore, muttered some more. Ron walked by the table. His father was reading the part about the Company accusing union officials from outside the place of interfering. "Interfering is exactly what they're doing."

"Just because they're offering support doesn't mean they're interfering," Ron said.

The old man looked up at him, eyeballs bulging out of their sockets. Beside himself, he thumped the table with his fist. "I tell you, if they keeps on like this, there'll be no jobs for anyone. They'll up and leave, that's what."

He started to wheeze. Ron looked at him hard,

at the throbbing vein on his temple. And his red face. Like he couldn't get his breath. Jeez. He wasn't going to have a heart attack or something, was he? He started coughing then and lurched towards the bathroom. Ron hung around outside the door. His own breath wasn't coming much easier than his father's.

When the hacking and rattling eased, Ron left. He passed his mother on the stairs. "Are you two at it again?"

"You should burn his bloody cigarettes."

She muttered, "...a bit late for that."

Okay...now what did that mean?

Ron threw himself on the bed and pushed a tape in the player. Even The Doors couldn't hammer away the uneasy feeling in the pit of his stomach.

6

FROM THE KITCHEN WINDOW, RON COULD SEE the familiar red and blue sweaters as both teams warmed up on the soccer field.

Grand Bank was playing. Not a game to miss. Ron wondered if Mac Follett would be in goal for them. He hoped not. Mac might have the face of a mackerel, but his arms and legs were like a squid's, all over the place. The ball seldom got past him.

Still about forty-five minutes before the game and the cars were already pulling in next to the railing that ran around the field.

Syl Stacey's green '65 Chevy was parked in the Church Lane, as usual. The old geezer had never paid to see a game in his life. And he had a prime view looking right down on the field. Not that he hadn't been razzed about it. Ron couldn't understand how anybody could be so tight. Duck said they should save the peels from the oranges the

team had at halftime and pelt Syl with them. Leave it to Duck to come up with something like that.

The stands were filling up pretty fast. Ron spotted the boys on the top bleacher. He couldn't miss them if he tried, not with the rowdy shouts coming from them. Ron waved to shut them up and climbed to the top level.

"I hope Bernie puts that whatshisname... Parsons, out of commission." Al's enthusiasm made his voice even louder. "Did you see how he tried to block Bernie's every move last week?"

"Where is he?" asked Duck, squinting across the field.

"Over there next to the Grand Bank goal," said Bert.

Ron turned up the collar of his windbreaker. "Looks like the mackerel's in goal, hey."

"Don't mean a thing," Bert said calmly. "They're nothing but a bunch of cod."

They all laughed. Not too often Bert cracked one.

Duck, not to be outdone, added, "And against us they're fish out of water."

Loud guffaws.

Amidst the laughing, Ron felt a tug at his knee. He looked down. On the bench below him sat Wayne. "Hey, Ron."

"Where'd you get the money to come to the game?" Ron asked.

"There's a hole in the fence," Wayne informed him.

"You snuck in?"

When Wayne didn't deny it, Ron said, "Mom'll be rory-eyed if she finds out, my son. Your best bet is to get out of here."

Al chuckled. "You're as bad as Syl over there in the lane, old man."

Wayne didn't budge. "You said I could come to the game with you sometime."

"That's right. Sometime. But not today."

"Yeah, Ron, just like you said you'd have a game with me."

Ron ignored him and eventually Wayne left.

Duck was still eyeing the lane where Syl was parked.

"Would you look at that? Some cheap, what? How can anybody be that cheap? You know what?" There was a wicked glint in his eye. "We should go collect from him…. Get the money box from the gatekeeper and go over there."

Ron laughed.

Bert shook his head. Duck and his crazy ideas.

But Al was right in there. He looked down over the back of the bleacher. "Yep, Johnny Bonnell is on the gate. He'll let us have the box."

Ron grinned. "Sure, I'll go."

Al was still looking down over the bleacher. He put his fingers to his mouth and whistled.

Ron looked too.

"Hey, Jacko," Al yelled.

Jackie, walking by in a string of girls, waved to Al.

"Didn't know you were so cosy with the brain," Ron said.

Al was still grinning. "She's nice, man. She lends me her notes. She even let me have her homework last week."

"What's with the name?"

"She's a nag. Like Bud Lake's old nag. Jacko."

"And she doesn't mind you calling her that?"

Al shrugged. "Never asked her. Here they come."

Jacko. Ron watched the group of girls until they found a spot to sit. Wonder what she'd say if he called her that? Jacko. He'd have to give it a try.

He turned his attention to the field for the kickoff.

When the ball went offside, Duck said to Ron, "Did you hear what Mick-Joe said to Nicole and her sister?"

Ron shook his head. He hadn't seen Nicole.

"He hucked a rock at them and said, 'Tell your old man that's the only spar he's taking out of here.'" Duck grinned.

Ron's eyes swept the bleachers. "Where are they?"

"Don't see them now. They were sitting down there." Duck tossed his head in the general direction of where he'd seen Nicole and her sister.

A cheer went up from the crowd. A goal! And Ron had missed it. He punched his fist hard into his hand.

"Did you see that?" Al slapped every back within arm's reach. "Sailed right in, it did. Perfect. That Tom still has the touch, what?"

Ron kept his eyes on the field for the rest of the period, but there were no more goals. Just lots of tense moments.

At halftime Duck said, "Okay, let's go collect."

Ron followed him off the bleacher. Al and Bert were right behind. They crossed the dirt parking lot, jumping potholes right and left.

Duck had no problem convincing Johnny to give them the money box, after he'd emptied it. "You sure this box is big enough for all he's going to give you?" Johnny joked.

The boys headed up the road and around the bend.

"I hope we get another goal or two in the next half," said Bert. "A little more insurance."

"I like it when it's close. More suspense," added Duck.

"Not me," said Al. "My nails are chewed down to the knuckles already. Even if our boys got a dozen goals, I'd be afraid the Grand Bankers would make a comeback in the next minute or so."

Ron laughed. He liked the suspense too. Well, no more than two goals for sure. He wanted the other team to have a fighting chance.

They were at the corner by the post office. Syl was just up the hill.

Bert hung back. "Who's going to ask him?"

"I think Ron should do it," said Duck.

Ron shoved him. Duck was so slight he just about went sprawling. "Why me?"

"Well, I had the idea," Duck said.

"That's right, Ron," said Al. "Fair is fair, old buddy." He grabbed the box from Duck's hand and shoved it at Ron.

Ron pushed it away. "No way, man," he said. "I'm not doing everything."

"All right, you big baby," goaded Al. "I'll hold the box, and you and Bert ask him. Give it here. You want me to hold your hand too?" And he burst out in a pitiful rendition of the Beatles song "I Wanna Hold Your Hand."

"I don't know what to say," said Bert. "Here, give me the box and you and Ron ask him."

"Good enough," said Al, passing it over.

They approached the car. The windows were up and Syl stared right past them. Al leaned in front of the windshield and saluted.

Syl's left eye twitched.

Ron tapped on the window.

Syl rolled it down an inch.

Duck grabbed Bert's hand and forced him to hold up the box.

Ron leaned close to the window. "Mr. Syl, sir, the boys and me, we were wondering, sir, if you'd like to donate to the gate, for the game, you know?" Mesmerized by the twitching eye, he ploughed on. "You know, sir, you have prime viewing here." There were titters behind him. He poked Al.

Al leaned closer, a stupid altar boy smile plastered on his silly face. "Yeah, and we had this idea. We're gonna see the town council about taking some of the proceeds from the gate to put up portable bleachers here in the lane and we thought, seeing as how you come here all the time, we thought we'd give you first chance, uh, to donate."

Syl never made a move.

Duck shoved Bert between Ron and Al. Al kept a straight face. "They might even have season tickets."

Holding the money box up to the window, Bert asked, "What do you think it'd be worth, sir?"

Ron leaned against the car door laughing hysterically. Syl rolled the window down, ever so slowly, till it was halfway. "What do I think it's worth?" he repeated. "This is what I thinks it's worth. Take this back with you." And he hawked a huge one, a huge green gob, that landed right on the front of Bert's jacket. Then he calmly raised the window.

Bert's face was stuck in shock for all of two seconds. Then it crumbled in dismay. Without a word he grabbed a handful of grass from the side of the road and wiped at his jacket. When Duck tried to help, Bert waved him aside, looking like he might take on anyone who came near.

Deliberately, with reddening face, he approached the car. He let out a godawful roar and pummelled the hood.

The boys cracked up. Tears ran down Al's face. Duck and Ron doubled over on the ground. Al tried to pull Bert off the old man's car but didn't have much luck until Ron got up and helped.

Ron and Al held Bert's arms till they were safely down the lane. Duck stayed out of his way. They managed to settle him down till he was only cursing and swearing at the old man, and at them.

Behind Bert's back, they grinned at each other. Bert wouldn't brag about this one.

They met up with Johnny on his way to lock

up the money. "Did you bring back some green ones?" he asked, taking the box from Al, who said, straight-faced, "Only one, but I don't think the bank would take it."

The boys doubled over laughing. Bert cursed them up in blue smoke and stalked off.

They crossed the parking lot, laughing so much they mucked right through the potholes. "Hey, Ron," Al said. "Isn't that Nicole? Over there, in the station wagon?"

Ron looked. Yep, that was her, slouched so far down in the driver's seat he could just see her head.

He smoothed his hair down, then sidled up and tapped the glass.

Nicole took her time looking to see who it was and then even longer to roll down the window. Her face was blotchy; she'd been crying.

He didn't know if he should let on that he noticed. "Is the game that bad?" Ron asked.

Nicole shook her head and made a weak attempt at a smile.

"Then what are you doing here when the two best teams on the Peninsula are playing?" Ron opened the car door. "Come on. That's enough of this."

Nicole got out and Ron slammed the door.

Now he'd have to sit with her. The boys had better not razz him. He'd take her to the far end of the bleachers.

Nicole pushed her hair off her face. "Ron, let's not go back to the game. Let's just walk."

A walk! When the Grand Bankers were playing! He was losing his mind. Plain and simple. He hoped the boys never found out about this.

Some chance. He and Nicole strolled across the strand behind the bleachers. Whistles and hoots followed them. Ron was glad they were too far away to make out the words.

"Those boys like teasing you," Nicole said as they walked up the incline onto the causeway.

"They'll stop after a bit when they see they're not getting to me."

There was a gleam in Nicole's eye. "Oh, you mean if we went out for a while, they'd stop?"

Ron knew he was pinkish and he hated it. "Something like that."

There was a sudden roar from the crowd, and car horns began blowing like crazy. Ron turned back to the field. The Laurentians had scored, and he'd missed it again! He wondered who had kicked it in. He jumped in the air and cheered.

"If you want to go back, it's okay."

"No, that's all right." What a lie.

She jammed her hands in her jeans pockets. "I'm never going to one of those games again."

"How come?" he asked, though he figured he knew already.

"That idiot, Mick somebody or other, says or does something every time he sees us."

"Ah, that's just Mick-Joe. Nobody listens to him."

"Then how come everybody laughed?" Nicole kicked at the ground with the toe of her sneaker.

Ron couldn't think of a reply. He looked across the harbour to where the *Hamildoc* was still docked. They walked in silence.

Then Nicole said, "Don't these people realize that without the Company there'd be no jobs here? They should be thankful for the work. A strike should be the last thing on their minds."

Ron looked at Nicole. He didn't care how pretty she was. He couldn't let that pass. "The Company should realize that without the miners they wouldn't be taking the big bucks out of here like they are."

Then he left her there on the causeway.

He felt petty afterwards, like he'd been fighting with his little sister or something. But somebody needed to set Nicole straight. He'd probably never see her again. He didn't care. Yes, he did.

On the way back to the soccer field, the whistle blew. Game over. In more ways than one, hey Ron.

7

"ONE THING YOU GOT TO UNDERSTAND IS this is not the first strike we've had here." Mr. Bennie's breath came in little pants.

Ron wondered if he should write that down. Probably not. Jackie wasn't.

Mr. Bennie stared out the window. He started to cough, as if the dismal grey sky were pressing on his chest and he couldn't get any relief. He didn't look too good and he sounded worse. Maybe he wasn't up to this.

Jackie was at the sink with a glass in her hand. "I'll get you a drink, Grandad."

Ron stifled a yawn. Jackie sent him a dirty look. He couldn't help it. Jeez, he was tired. Besides, he'd been here a half-hour already and didn't have one word on his paper. He'd expected to be half done by now. Ron resigned himself to a long evening. He tried for a more comfortable position on the hard chair.

Mr. Bennie gripped the arms of the green recliner. His hands were wasted and grey. Like the rest of him, they had been coated in mine dust too often, for too many years. Finally, the coughing spasm eased. Jackie held the glass to his lips and he sipped.

He settled back again and closed his eyes for a few seconds. Then he looked at Ron. "They takes good care of me. I can hardly walk across a room anymore, let alone drive. So they got me this chair." Mr. Bennie smiled affectionately at Jackie. "I can live out my days going up and down." He pulled the lever on the side and sat up straighter. "This is my mine shaft now, eh, Jackie girl?" A pained smile touched his face.

"Now, Grandad, don't talk like that." Jackie set the glass on the windowsill within his reach.

Ron shifted uncomfortably. How long did they expect him to stay?

Mr. Bennie continued as if there hadn't been an interruption. "Yes, over the years there's been more than a few strikes." He rested his head on the chair back. "In 1939 the Union was formed, and a good thing too."

"Why, Grandad?"

"My dear child, the working conditions were something terrible." He stopped talking.

Ron could hear each breath he drew.

"In the early years there'd be shutdowns in the mine. If it wasn't a broken part, it was problems with the power. Low water in the dams in summer or line trouble with storms in winter. No such thing as emergency power then." He took his time. "Lots of times men had to swim to their waists trying to save the pumps...and then...for want of a place to dry out...had to stay wet until they walked home." Mr. Bennie shook his head remembering.

Ron and Jackie waited, unwilling to interrupt his thoughts.

"And the wages...deplorable, considering it was the hardest kind of work a man could do." He paused.

"What was the pay, Grandad?"

"The pay? Fifteen cents an hour."

Ron dropped the ballpoint he was twirling.

The look again. Ron was getting used to it.

Mr. Bennie wiped his forehead with a white hanky.

"But it was better than the dole."

Ron picked up the pen. "Pretty tough to build up a bank account at that rate."

Mr. Bennie massaged his thigh and winced. "A bank account? My sonny boy, there were times the men didn't get paid at all." He looked from Ron to Jackie. "Not one copper." Another pause. "For instance, if a piece of equipment arrived at the wharf and duty had to be paid on it, the men would have to forego their wages, so's the Company could pay the duty. That happened more than once."

"Could they do that?" Ron asked, incredulous. "How'd they get away with it?"

Mr. Bennie smiled. A tired smile. "There was no other work to be had." He sipped the water. "St. Lawrence was never a stranger to hard times. Right from day one. The first settlers were a crew of shipwrecked sailors."

Jackie cut in. "One of the men was named Richard Clarke, right, Grandad?"

Ron looked at her. She already knew all this stuff. "So that means Pete Clarke in our class...his father is Richard Clarke...they must be related, I mean, descended from them sailors?" He was proud of himself for making the connection.

Jackie nodded, impatient to move on. "I thought everyone knew that."

Ron shook his head slowly. "Not me." Course he hadn't really been researching it either. And among the boys he hung around with it had just never come up.

Mr. Bennie, between sips of water and little rests, talked for quite a while. It wasn't hard to listen to really, the way he told it.

"Times were hard, I tell you. There was no

such thing as new clothes. Even flour bags were used, to make underwear. You'd see them hanging on the line and you could still make out the brand name, Five Roses or Cream of the West." Mr. Bennie chuckled.

So did Ron. That was pretty good.

Even Jackie grinned. She hadn't cracked a smile all evening. She was put out about something. Moving too slow for her probably. Every time her grandad told a little story she fidgeted and doodled on her page. Let her. Ron didn't care. The stories were the parts he liked.

Jackie switched on the light. "You must be getting tired, Grandad?"

"A bit, yes."

Ron closed his binder. "Were you around for the tidal wave, Mr. Bennie?"

"Indeed I was. To the day I die I'll remember Tommy Pike's horse bolting for the backwoods. You never saw a creature go so fast." He shook his head, smiled, and took his time before he went on, like he was reliving the whole thing. "They said at the time that he went out on the tide with the barn and back in with the next rush of water. Whatever happened, the poor thing wasn't seen for three days." Mr. Bennie laughed his soundless, wheezing laugh. He wiped his watery eyes with the hanky before he went on. "I was standing on the waterfront, or what was left of it. When he ripped past me, I could feel his terror. Jacko was his name."

Ron burst out laughing. So that's where the name came from. "That's some story, sir."

Jackie was as pink as the geranium on the windowsill. Ron's grin was innocent. "When would be a good time to come again?"

"Tomorrow evening, if you can make it. No soccer game, is there?"

Ron shook his head. "Not till Thursday."

Jackie was hidden behind the open fridge door when he went out.

Softly Ron said, "See you, Jacko."

From the fridge came a muffled, "Drop dead."

Once he was outside, his grin erupted in a laugh, a good loud hoot. Jackie, with her head stuffed in the fridge. Drop dead. He laughed again. He should have pulled the fridge door wide. Maybe not. He grinned. No sense in making her really mad at him.

He whistled as he jogged across the field. He vaulted over a boggy spot, without getting his sneakers wet. "Tarrant, you're a god," he said aloud and took a little run to jump the brook, easily sailing across. Funny how the brook had seemed so big when he was small and used to catch grasshoppers there. He slowed to a walk

and came up to the road.

His father's truck was in the yard. Ron didn't feel like going home yet. Didn't want to lose his good mood. He tucked the binder between the fence slats so that it rested on the bottom piece of two-by-four and, without glancing towards the house, headed down the harbour. Might as well see if anything was happening on the picket line.

A breeze was starting to pick up. It stirred the flurry of dark clouds skulking around the Cape and whipped them in across the harbour. Rain before too long. Didn't bother Ron. He was used to it. All the fog and rain must be hard on people from away, used to sunshine day after day. Like Nicole. He'd get tired of that, squinting at that sun for days at a time. He'd rather have it this way.

Nicole had looked at him today like she wanted to talk. But he didn't go near. He wanted to, but didn't have anything to say. Maybe in a few more days, after they both forgot what happened. Thinking of her now, he wanted to forget fast.

Ron could see the silhouettes of people below the road, sitting on rocks and humps of ground. In the background, the fluorspar and the *Hamildoc* were black shadows between grey sky and water.

Halfway down the bank a few women were

singing, fitting their own words to a Newfoundland folk song. They laughed as much as they
sang. Ron listened.

We don't want yer maggoty offer.
We'll stay out all winter.
We can get better than that
if we all stick together.

Ron hummed the chorus; there was no one
close enough to hear. He liked to sing, but hadn't
been able since he turned thirteen and his voice
changed and his hair went curly. He wondered if
the two were related.

He looked around. Was that Bert down there
with those men? Who were they anyway? He
strolled down the hill. Yep. That was Bert all
right, sitting on the edge of the group.

There was Bill Slaney, Jerry Tobin, Sam Beck,
Gar Haskell. All miners, or strikers now. All
young fellows too, except for Gar. Jerry and Sam
weren't even married yet, though Jer would be
soon, the way he was always hugged up to Stella
Lake.

Since the incident with old Syl, Ron had
stayed out of Bert's way. The men were talking, so
Ron kicked his foot. Bert looked up and nodded.
He edged back. "How's it going, buddy?"

"Not bad," Ron replied, squatting on his heels. He turned down the drag Bert offered him. Bert was smoking in the open now. He looked around for Bert's parents. No sign of them. Still, Ron was impressed. Until he noticed that Bert held the smoke hidden in his fist ready to flick it aside in a sec. Maybe Bert wasn't so open after all.

The miners' talk was lively.

Bert turned back to them. Ron listened too.

"Why can't they just have the vote and get it over with?" Jer spat a bit of tobacco from his home-rolled cigarette. "No one is going to be retarded enough to accept a dollar twenty-three an hour over two years."

Except my old man. Ron wanted to leave, sneak off without a soul noticing. But he couldn't. His big feet decided all on their own to put down roots here, deep ones holding him to the spot.

"Didn't you hear whatshisname, aw, I can't think of it...he's a Company spokesman...." Sam waved his smoke in the air, strewing ashes over everyone.

"Elliot." Bert supplied the name.

Up went Sam's arm again. "That's him. On the radio this morning he said that some miners are saying privately they wants to accept –"

Bill cut in. "Aw, don't listen to that bull. They'll say that, just to try and stir up trouble.

Divide and conquer, that's one of their tactics."

"C'mon Bill, are you trying to tell me that some of those older fellas are happy about us being off this long?" Sam asked. "Fellas like Johnnie Lockyer, Fred Loder, Har Reeves? They're within a few years of retiring, close to getting pensioned off." Sam's laugh was bitter. "And getting the gold watch."

Ron was sure they were going to bring up his old man's name any second. He felt the tip of his ears burn. He waited.

Sam punched Gar on the shoulder. "What about you, Skipper? Are you looking forward to the gold watch?"

Gar shook his head. "A few years to go yet," he said in his quiet way.

Ron contemplated rolling down the hill to the landwash. The small waves slapping the shore would feel good on his hot cheeks.

Then Stella waltzed over, her eyes locked on Jer. Good thing Jer didn't mind, because it was clear he didn't have a chance. Ron scrabbled back to make room for her. She walked right to Jer and took his arm, pulling him up off the grass. "Come on, sweetie, we're taking my mom to bingo in Lawn, remember?" She lowered her voice. "Isn't that Richard Walsh coming this way? Yes, it is. He must be back from St. John's."

Stella worked in the hospital, so she knew everyone's personal business.

No one answered her, because Richard was right there.

His wife was with him. "Grand evening," Richard said.

"Finest kind," Gar agreed. He stood up. "How's things going? You looks the best kind."

Richard nodded. "I feels good. Eats good too. That's all you can ask for, I s'pose."

It was Gar's turn to nod.

Mrs. Maizie looked at Gar. You could tell she was upset. "You can't go by a man's looks." To her husband she said. "You mustn't be feeling that good. You been spitting up blood every day since you come out of the hospital."

There wasn't a stir from anyone. Those with cigarettes in hand stared at the ash and the rest at the ore carrier in the harbour.

Richard shifted on the uneven ground. "Oh, I knows I'm getting worse. Gradual. More shortness of breath. And the awful burning in my stomach. But the doctor tells me I'm good for a while yet." He paused. "That's it, by. What can you do?"

They moved on.

Jer shook his head. "Another one." He flicked his cigarette away and stood up, draping his arm over Stella's shoulder.

"Yes, and he won't be the last," Stella said.

Jer squeezed her shoulder. "Hey, settle down."

"Open your eyes, dear. There's been five died just in the past year and a half. And they're still getting sick."

No one spoke. The men pulled hard on their smokes, as if it was the only thing that mattered.

Ron got up too, figuring he would make his getaway.

This was too depressing.

"How's your dad doing?" Gar asked. "I haven't seen him around."

Ron felt himself shrivel till he was as small as the fire on the tip of Jer's smoke. Was Gar just trying to change the subject? How was his old man? Miserable as ever or more — that's what he was. Or was Gar trying to make some kind of dig? Let him, he didn't care. Ron wasn't about to stick up for his father. Gar was looking at him. He didn't know what to say. His old man was probably home hawking his guts up. Or nursing a hangover. And he really didn't want to tell Gar that. He should have taken off as soon as he got here, when he heard what they were talking about.

Ron shrugged. "He's around."

"Didn't see him on the picket line today," said Gar.

"I dunno," said Ron. Jeez, he had to get out of here. He stood up, thankful when Bert ground his cigarette under his heel and joined him to walk up the hill to the road.

But tonight Bert was even more full of himself than usual. He rambled on about why the Union hadn't taken a vote. Ron wasn't listening.

Then Bert said something about the Brook boys – and Mick-Joe. Mick-Joe? "What did you say?"

"I don't boil my cabbage twice."

Bert could be really irritating. "Come on, tell me. What about the Brook boys?"

"I just said I heard Mick-Joe and his gang talking. It sounded like they were going after the Brook boys."

"Which Brook boys?"

Bert scoffed. "Which Brook boys – well now, there's not that many, is there?"

"Where did you hear that?"

"I stopped at Dudler's on my way to the picket. Mick-Joe and his boys were there. I was pretty sure that's what they were talking about."

"When are they gonna go after them?"

"Dunno."

"Where?"

"Don't know that either."

"Aw, Mick-Joe's all talk. Probably won't do nothing."

"Maybe so, maybe not. But if I was them I'd watch out."

"We should warn them," Ron urged.

"We? Not me, buddy. I'm staying out of it."

"Jeez man, we just can't let Mick-Joe and his gang get them. For no good reason."

"Who says they haven't got a good reason?"

"Well, what is it then?"

"The strike, that's what."

Ron was flabbergasted. "Sure, the strike's not their fault. They can't help that."

Bert shrugged. "We can't help it either. That's just the way it is, Ron."

"You don't mean that, Bert. You like them fellows too. What about Paul? And Danny?"

"That was before. It's different now."

"Doesn't have to be."

Bert shook his head. "Do you know what side you're on, Ron?" He turned to go down the harbour. Then he stopped and looked back. "You better."

Ron swore, all the way home. At Bert, Mick-Joe, the strike, his old man. The whole blasted lot.

The truck was gone from the yard this time. Probably over at the club. Its other home.

"How come Dad didn't go on the picket line today?" Ron asked.

Mom stood at the sink. She scrubbed at the cuff of a school shirt and didn't look up. "He had

to go see the doctor."

"Why? What happened?"

"Nothing happened, Ron. He just went to see the doctor, that's all."

Was she ever touchy this evening. Ron persisted. "What for? What did the doctor say?"

"He's got to go to St. John's."

"St. John's. What for?" he asked. He was practically on her back, she was speaking so softly.

An exasperated sigh. "Some tests."

She was stalling. Their own hospital handled the regular stuff, but when you got sent to St. John's it was for more complicated things. When Miss Doyle, the music teacher, fell down the concrete steps at school a couple years ago and did something to her back, the helicopter landed in the harbour and took her to St. John's. And little Hammer Miller, who lived just behind their house, had to have his sixth toe removed in St. John's just last fall.

"I know what it is. It's that coughing, isn't it?"

She didn't deny it. He was right. He knew it.

He hoped the doctors would check the nicotine buildup in his lungs. They'd probably need a pressure hose to flush them out.

8

MR. FARRELL SCRAWLED THEIR MATH HOME-work on the board and left, eight minutes early. Before class Al had moved the clock ahead. Even if Mr. Farrell knew, he wouldn't care all that much, as long as it didn't happen every day and make him look bad.

Ron's grin was easy. It was one of those rare times when school wasn't such a bad place to be. Of course, it could change just like that with Perky Pat swooping down on them, hustling the rabble back to their seats. But for the time being, everything was just fine.

The room got disarranged fast. The straight rows of desks were the first to go. Then the plants on the wide windowsill got shoved to the far end, and several boys took over the space. Ron was one of them.

He hooked his heels on the bookshelf below and felt the books give way. Duck was telling Ron about the wrestling match on TV between Abdullah the Butcher and some guy who didn't even last two rounds.

Out of the corner of his eye Ron saw Al, sitting on the desk in front of him, chuck a pen top to the front of the room. Ron turned his head, curious to see Al's target.

Jackie turned around from the group of girls she was gabbing with and brushed the top of her head. "Hey, stop that," she called to Al, the corners of her mouth twitching.

Al beckoned. "Come here for a sec."

Jackie shook her head in pretend annoyance but came back to see what Al wanted.

Ron had stopped listening to Duck.

"Sit down," Al commanded. "I want to talk to you."

She perched on the desk next to Al. "If it's notes you want, the answer is no." She laughed. "I'm not your secretary."

So, she could laugh when she wanted to. Imagine that. And Al was lapping it up. Too bad he hadn't seen her miserable side like Ron had. He caught himself glaring at them.

Jackie didn't even glance Ron's way. That was all right. It gave him a chance to watch her. Figure her out.

Al said, "Remember that tape you promised me?"

Jackie shook her head. "What tape?"

Al grabbed her wrist and burst into song. "Stayin' alive, stayin' alive...."

She laughed. "Oh, the Bee Gees. I'll bring it tomorrow."

Ron couldn't stop himself. He jumped off the window ledge. "I wouldn't lend him anything if I were you. You'll never get it back."

"Whadaya mean, buddy? I gave you back your tapes."

"Yeah, a year later you did."

Jackie laughed. "Oh, then maybe I won't bring it after all." She struggled to get out of Al's grip.

"Come on," Al said.

"Maybe." She pulled free and rubbed her wrist. "Now look what you did."

Before Al had a chance to reply Donna came over. She was Jackie's best friend. "Jackie, I have to babysit this evening. Want to come over and do homework?"

Ron looked at Jackie. They were both supposed to meet with her grandfather that evening.

Jackie shook her head quickly. When she spoke, the words came out like an embarrassing spill. "No, I'm sorry, I can't, not this evening."

"How come?" Donna asked.

"Grandad is helping me with my assignment."

Ron hopped up on the ledge again. Grandad

was helping her, was he? What about Ron? He leaned against the windowpane and crossed his arms. He felt like asking Jackie what time he should be there. Felt like it, but he didn't.

Marlene came along and ruffled Al's hair. Nicole was with her.

Al jumped up, boxing the air, as if to take her on. "Don't touch the 'do,' woman, don't touch the 'do.'"

Nicole laughed at Al, but she smiled straight at Ron. "Anyone going to the softball game this evening?"

There was a chorus of "me, me" from the boys on the window ledge.

Nicole pulled on the leg of Ron's jeans. "What about you?"

"I might," he said, grinning like an idiot.

The sight of Perky in the doorway wiped the grin right off his face though.

The crowd dispersed and straightened their desks. Jackie muttered as she slipped past Ron, "I'll tell Grandad you can't make it."

Ron followed her. "Tell him what you like. That's your style, isn't it?"

He knew he'd gotten to her when he saw how her back stiffened. Served her right. He was glad he'd said it. No, he wasn't. He felt like a jerk. He plunked himself in his desk, hitting his hip bone as he did. He swore. Jeez, nothing was working out. He got up and asked to leave the room.

As Ron pushed open the bathroom door Nipper Beck, in grade seven, was making a fast exit. The front of his shirt was soaking wet. "What happened to you, buddy?" Ron asked. "Go for a dip in the toilet?"

Nipper's eyes bulged from their sockets. "Cyril Roul sprayed me," he sputtered.

Ron went in. Yep. There was Cyril aiming for the ceiling with a soggy wad of paper towel in his hand. Cyril was one of Mick-Joe's sidekicks, a pain if ever there was one.

"Hey, Tarrant. Got a smoke?"

"Nope." He wouldn't give Cyril a smoke if he had a whole carton.

The door opened and in came Danny, his fingers full of ink. "Hey, Ron." Danny headed for the sink. "My blasted pen broke," he said in his mainland accent.

Cyril blocked his way. "Well now, Brook boy, this sink's in use. You'll have to go somewhere else."

Ron could tell Danny was taken by surprise, but he recovered quickly. He shoved Cyril aside. "Get out of my way."

Cyril shoved back, slamming Danny against the wall.

Ron grimaced. That was close. Danny had just

missed hitting his head on the metal edge of the paper towel holder.

Danny came back at Cyril, leaving ink smears on Cyril's shirt.

Cyril grunted with that last shove and looked at his shirt. His face went purple. He charged at Danny. Tried to get him in a headlock. But Danny was too slippery.

Ron watched, ready to intervene if Danny needed help. So far he was doing okay.

Then weasel-faced Lar, another of Cyril and Mick-Joe's cronies, popped out of the cubicle. Didn't even flush the toilet. Lar's lip curled at the sight of Danny in Cyril's clutches. There was a nasty gleam in his eyes.

Ron, half a foot taller, stepped in front of Lar. He put a hand, fingers spread, on Lar's scrawny chest. "In case you got any ideas – forget it."

The bathroom door swung open and the principal stormed in. Nipper must have gone right to him. "What's going on here?"

Cyril stepped back. Danny turned on the tap. Neither said a word.

"Come with me," the principal ordered. He looked at Ron and Lar, standing side by side. "Are you in on this too?"

"It's nothing to do with them," Danny said, heading out the door.

Ron gave Lar a dirty look and followed the others out. By the time he returned to class, her royal perkiness had taken centre stage. With a captive audience there was no stopping her. She waved her arms, and the broad black sleeves retreated to her elbows. She approached the board with a flourish. HISTORY, she printed in large block letters.

Perky paused and glanced around the room. No reaction. Then she added a slash and in more block letters the word HERSTORY.

A few giggles, from the girls.

She charged across the front of the room, her nun garb flapping off the first desk in each row, executed a wide turn, and ended up back at the board again where she ran her hand under the words, stopping under HERSTORY. Eyeballing the boys, she said, "You didn't think you had the monopoly on this branch of knowledge, did you?"

Ron hove up his hand. "Well, Sister," he said, with all the earnestness he could muster, "the name says it all. It wouldn't be called his story for nothing now, would it?" He looked to the boys around him for support. "Eh, fellas?"

Duck hooted. "Man, you've had it. You're dead meat."

The girls, bent on giving the women their

rightful place in history, or herstory, got down-right dirty. They dragged up every famous woman they could think of, even the saints.

Ron slid down in his desk as far as he could and put his hand up to shield himself from the assault. It was almost as much fun as the break, before Perky came on the scene.

It was Donna, Jackie's friend, who surprised them. "You might think this is all a bit of fun," she said in a nervous, but deadly voice. "But I'll tell you one thing...." She paused. "If I had a choice between living my dad's life and my mom's, I'd choose my dad's anytime. Dad works his shift and then he's off to the club or some-where, but Mom works all day at the shop, comes home, cooks supper, does housework half the night, and looks after seven youngsters besides."

Ron nodded. He couldn't agree more.

Sister intervened then. "This issue of equality is an excellent one to discuss, and I hope you'll give it more thought. But it's not what I had in mind for today." She moved to perch on the edge of the desk. "Though it serves very well to make the point, and that is, that there is more than one side to a story." She paused. "Sometimes there are many sides. Let's take the term *history*. We've always thought of it as a record of past events. But have you ever stopped to think whose record? She hopped off the edge of the desk. "Let's look at another definition." She wrote on the board, talking as she formed the letters. "History: the acts, ideas, or events that will or can shape the course of the future." She turned to them. "Have you ever thought of history as events happening now that can shape the future?" Sister waited for her words to sink in.

Ron was hungry. It must be close to lunchtime. He felt like telling her that if she had a point to make, get to it. Time was running out. Especially with Al's timekeeping. One day last week, she'd kept them a full five minutes after the bell. Perky must have read his mind because she said, "We have about twenty minutes before lunch."

Not so, Ron contradicted her in his mind. Seventeen minutes and a few seconds. He sighed. Overtime again.

Perky went on. "Our topic of discussion this morning is the strike." There was a collective gulp, inaudible and deafening at the same time.

But Sister felt it too. She paused, unsure of herself for a moment. Took the *perky* right out of her. Then she ploughed on, stumbling through the smothering silence that filled the room. "I want you to discuss it in terms of its impact on the town, present *and* future. I'd also like you to consider the different perspectives people have. You know, the strike will never be resolved unless both sides get together and talk. Right? That's a given. Well, it's the same in the classroom. And in your life. As caring, compassionate human beings, we need to talk through the issues we come up against in our lives, no matter how difficult."

Didn't this nun get it? Nobody wanted to talk about the strike. It was bad enough having to deal with it out there. Why drag all this up in school? Ron was fed up. Man, this Perky – she didn't know a thing.

Now she was trying to break them into groups. "All I want you to do," she said, "is to come up with as many points of view towards the strike as you can."

Ron dropped his chin in his hands and surveyed the room. Jackie doodled on her notebook. She was making no move to join a group. Donna twisted the pencil in her hands. She wasn't in a group. Duck had his hand over his mouth muttering something to Bert across the aisle. And Al had bent his ruler in a perfect arc; Ron waited for it to snap. Nobody in a group near Al either. And Nicole. With her head down, her hair hiding her face.

Ron looked at Perky, hands on her hips...did nuns have hips...whatever...at the front of the room. Perky threw up her arms in despair. "All right, let's do it together on the board."

Silence. Then Bert grunted. "The only side I'm taking is the one I'm on."

The old perkiness was back. "Fine, Bert. What should I write? the union? the miners? the strikers?"

Another grunt. "Same thing."

She bestowed an accommodating smile on him and waited. The whole thing reminded Ron of the old tale of the spider and the fly. And Bert sure seemed to him to be the fly, walking right into her sticky web.

Before long Perky got what she was waiting for. Yep. From Marlene, who'd do anything for a smile like Bert just got. "My dad is on strike too." She flashed her made-up eyes at Bert before basking in Sister's attention. "But Sister, he won't have anything to do with that Union. He says they're all troublemakers."

Ron groaned inwardly. He rubbed his hand over his face. His old man and Marlene's. Two good ones together all right. He wanted out of here. Seven minutes left. If Perky didn't notice the clock was fast.

Sister retreated to the board. "I think maybe we'd better make two lists. She had a purposeful look on her face now, like she felt she was getting somewhere.

The back of Bert's neck was a dull red. He wasn't

used to being done in. And the fact that it was Marlene made it worse. He'd asked her out a while ago but she'd laughed in his face. Everyone knew that Marlene only dated Brook boys. Too bad for Bert though.

Jackie put up her hand. Ron listened in spite of himself. "A lot of miners do support the Union." Her voice was even, steady, like she was making an effort to keep her feelings out of it.

Ron's anger at her melted in his chest, slipped down to his gut like a blob of dissolving jelly. Someone needed to cancel out Marlene. He never thought it would be Jackie though. In a weird way he was kind of proud of her. As if he had a right. She couldn't even speak a civil word to him.

Sister nodded. "Thank you, Jackie." She scribbled gleefully on the board, talking steadily. "Why don't I write 'Miner/Pro-Union' and 'Miner/Anti-Union?'" There was a perky glow about her now.

After that, the responses came right and left. No comment, though, from the third seat in the row by the door. Nicole, chin in hand, was still hunched over her desk. She must have memorized every grain of wood by now. Ron felt sorry for her. She was outnumbered here, twenty-two to one.

In a sense, he and Nicole were in the same

boat. The thought was cold comfort. Neither of them wanted this "perky discussion." For different reasons, of course. Ron didn't know about Nicole, but he felt like he was heading out to sea – without a paddle.

Donna's hand was up again. She said her mom was worried she might lose her job at Farrell's store if business got much worse.

And Sheila Quirke mentioned sick miners, adding that her Uncle Joe had died last year from the miner's disease.

Ron fidgeted. The discussion swirled inside his head.

His knee jiggled a mile a minute and he cracked his knuckles just as fast. How many more idiotic points of view could they come up with? There were only about two thousand people in the whole town. Did every bloody one of them have a point of view?

He wished these guys would just shut up. Didn't they know what time it was? He eyed the clock. Eleven forty-five on the dot. "Lunchtime," he announced, loud, way too loud.

Heads turned. Ron's face and neck were past red now. Crimson was the word to describe his colour. Bright crimson. He shoved his books in his desk. Around him there were a few chuckles. Al, Duck, and Bert started to unwind from their desks, grinning thankfully in his direction.

Sister glanced at the clock over the blackboard. "I guess it is time to wrap up for today. Thank you, Ron, for being the timekeeper."

Al winked.

"My pleasure, Sister. Anytime." A bob of the head. God, he was sweating.

9

"**B**RING ME SOMETHING? DAD? BRING ME something?" Carrie shook her father's legs. They were slung along the end of the table, feet sticking out. Her mother went around them to set out the plates for lunch.

"Da-a-d?" Carrie's voice was as rhythmic as her shaking. Her brown eyes were intent on her dad's face.

He stared out the window as oblivious to her as if she'd been a fly on his pant leg. Their father was the easiest on Carrie. She got away with stuff he wouldn't dream of doing.

"Carrie, stop that. Go get the butter," her mom said.

Ron gently pulled a curl. Carrie slapped his hand. "Dad's going to St. John's and he's going to bring me something." Without slacking off on the shaking, she added hopping to her routine.

Ron looked at his mother. She was worried all right.

She thought she was hiding it, but it was written all over her face. The closed look and the tightness around her mouth couldn't hold it. The worry seeped out through her eyes.

"If he brings you something, he has to bring me something too." Wayne plunked himself on the chair at the other end of the table and reached for a slice of bread. "Mom, you told Carrie to bring the butter."

Suddenly their father uncoiled himself. Towering over them, he hissed, "Yes-s-s. That's what I'm going to do in there, shop for presents. A bloody holiday is what this is."

Carrie figured this was a good time to get the butter. Their father reeled across the kitchen. "Perhaps I'll bring back a big box and some nails and ye can all help hammer the lid."

Ron sighed in disgust. It was just like the old man, always seeing the worst.

Wayne and Carrie buttered their bread, having already tuned him out. Their mother put her hand to her mouth, as if by covering her own she could silence his.

Ron wanted to put his arms around her. But he couldn't. No telling what Himself would do if he took it the wrong way. Best to do nothing till the storm passed.

His dad opened a beer. The opener clattered

into the sink.

"Leo...the doctor said...."

Ron groaned and dropped his head to the table. Didn't she know when to leave well enough alone?

"Leo..." mimicked his father, his mouth ugly. "The doctor said.... The doctor is a young, know-nothing pup."

Carrie giggled, and covered her mouth.

Ron's look shut her up.

Finally, beer in hand, the old man went to watch the news.

The smell of the Franco-American canned spaghetti heating on the stove turned Ron's stomach.

"Ron, there's some hash here too."

He ate. Only because it was easier than not eating.

Not going to school was also easier than going. And not go was what Ron did. He didn't even have to weigh the pros and cons. There were no cons. Only pros. After this morning at school and noon at home, it was time out.

He couldn't have picked a better afternoon if he'd ordered it up himself. One of those prairie days must have snuck clear across the country, and Ron liked the look of it. The sky was blue like he'd seldom seen and stretching up to heaven. If there was one. On top of that, the afternoon was warm, comfortably warm, kitchen warm.

Though some kitchens could be pretty cold places at times. But he wasn't going to think about that now.

In bright sunlight and in broad view, right in the middle of the road when there were no cars coming, Ron strolled down the harbour, destination unknown. Just past Kelly's stage he chucked a rock into the harbour and felt himself begin to unwind.

The tide was out. He scrabbled down the bank to the landwash and stayed there for a while, content to pick his way around fish stages, eyes peeled for the right size throwing rock. Then he would wind up and let go. Mainlanders said stones. Nobody from the place did though.

Did the Brook boys say stones? Ron couldn't remember.

He was careful not to aim close to any of the dories or skiffs out on their moorings. The men wouldn't put up with that. Ron's distance was steadily improving and so were his spirits. Out there was the *Hamildoc*, a pockmark on the harbour. He aimed for it. Too far.

Some time later he heard laughter and guitar playing and looked up the bank to see the women. Ron strolled towards them. He knew everyone. None of the boys' mothers were there. No nosy questions.

They were mostly young wives, probably taking the afternoon shift while their young ones were in school. There was no doubt that everyone here was on the same side. Ron felt himself unwinding a bit more. No one spoke to him directly, but the smiles were friendly. No one asked why he wasn't in school. No one mentioned his old man.

He ambled past the small groups. The talk ranged from recipes to the soaps and makeup, and lots of laughing, at their husbands' expense mostly. Off to the side the songwriters practised.

Someone called his name. It was Gina Lambert, Al's auntie. "Ron, would you run over and get us four Cokes?"

"Sure."

"Keep one for yourself. And listen, honey..."

Ron blushed. She wasn't all that old, and she was pretty too.

"...after you bring the Cokes, you'll have to move on. We can't have anyone underage here during the day."

Sara Slaney gave him a kind smile. "We don't want to give them anything to use against us. You can come back this evening for a while if you like."

Ron nodded. He understood.

Later, taking long swigs of Coke, he wandered farther down the harbour. Fish stages, shops, and storage sheds, in various states of disrepair, made up the bulk of the buildings. There were even a few houses built below the road, right next to their stages.

On Ron's right was a boarded-up shop, its white paint grunged by years of salt spray. At least you could see what the salt did to things. Not like the mine dust. Richard Walsh, walking around with his wife the other evening, looked fine on the outside. It was his insides the dust gnawed away.

Too bad that little shop closed. When Ron was about ten he bought his mother's Christmas present there. It still hung on the wall in the front room, a ceramic vase with ferns. He had to pay extra for the ferns and he was short a nickel, but Mrs. Annie had let him have it anyway.

Ron passed Farrell's grocery store, and Aylward's run-down clapboard place that stored caskets. The uneven double doors were nailed shut with just a piece of two-by-four. But then, who would bother with a place like that? It would be bad enough to go there if a person had to.

He looked out at the harbour. Yes, some place this was. The salt was slowly but surely corroding the town and the dust doing more or less the same thing to the people.

He was in The Dock now. Shingle Point jutted out into the harbour on his left and on the right the dock road curved uphill. Ron took neither. He walked straight ahead, past the last few houses and Lake's old restaurant, up the incline, and onto the path to Blue Beach.

He looked across the harbour to Herring Cove on the other side, a sight pretty enough for a post-card. Stages under the banks stuck out in the cove, bandy-legged, with their dories on moorings. Above the banks, a smattering of houses scattered in a stretch of meadow that sloped down to the shore. Ron threw back his head and filled his lungs with the sea air.

He had walked here so many times he could do it with his eyes closed, except that it wouldn't be too smart. The narrow footpath through scruffy low-lying juniper ran not even a foot from the edge of a sharp drop down to sheer rock below. Nobody fooled around here. Though he and the boys had once tried to climb the granite wall this side of Blue Beach. They made it halfway till they ran into a cliff face as smooth as a sheet of plywood and had to inch their way back down.

It had been a couple years ago, but Ron bristled at the thought of what happened after. He and his buddies had been on their way home. It was late, but not quite dark, when Ron spotted the green pickup. The old man had come looking for him. His father jumped out of the truck, fist up, ready to nail Ron. Ron hopped into the back, out of reach of his father's long arm. Later, at home, his mother had shielded him from his father's belt.

Ron remembered the feeling of powerlessness and wishing he was bigger, stronger. The old man wouldn't try that now.

Ron had wished his father was dead. That time, and other times. It seemed his father was always after him about something or other. Not just lately. All his life. Any memory he had was about getting a licking, or barely escaping one. There was the time he removed all the fuses from the fuse box and gave them to Cal Pittman up the hill so Cal would let him play. Mom went to get supper and there was no power. He got his behind warmed and was put to bed for that one.

Another time, he took Gary Haskell's bike from the side of the road while Gary was in Bill's shop, buying bubble gum, and he ran smack into a car. Didn't hurt Ron or the bike but made a long scratch down the side of Paul Turpin's new car. Paul came right to the door and told. Another licking.

He couldn't recall any good times with his

father. The old man certainly never kicked the ball around with Ron. For one thing he was hardly ever home. Except to eat, sleep, and watch the news. And dish out lickings. The rest of the time he was working or at the club.

Now Ron might get his wish. Did he really mean it? There were a lot of good things about having the old man gone and not many about having him around. No, sir, not many. Mom would probably miss him. And Carrie too. Not Wayne though. Not much anyway. He never played ball with Wayne either. Ron felt a twinge of discomfort at the thought. As far as kicking ball with Wayne went, he wasn't much better than the old man.

And Ron? Would he miss his father? He didn't know. He really didn't know. Life would be more pleasant without being picked on all the time. But it would probably be tougher too. How would Mom look after them?

He jumped the couple of feet down over the bank and landed on a shelf of rock at the edge of the beach. In front of him was the broken rusted hull of a whaler that had run ashore years before. Ron tossed shards of rock at it, listening for the pinging sounds as they hit.

The harbour here, sheltered by the Cape, was as calm as a pond. Tiny beach rocks and broken shells, caught in the ripples at the water's edge, tumbled and rolled in what little bit of surf there was. Ron found himself listening for the next little rocky slap on the shore.

He stooped to pick up a round blue rock. Something whistled past his head, pinged the iron hull, and ricocheted against a rock behind him.

Ron jumped. "Hey, watch out," he yelled, clambering over the rocks, waving his arms. What kind of a crazy fool....

Mick-Joe. On the bank, BB gun under his arm. He swaggered even when he wasn't moving.

Ron straightened up and kept his mouth shut. Mick-Joe and a gun. Not a good combination.

Mick-Joe looked at Ron. Then his nutso loon laugh echoed across the water. He strode down the rock slabs, letting out a string of swears the length of the beach, at the end of which he said, "Schoolboy, when I wants to hit you, you'll know it. Why don't you wear a red flag or something?" He glanced around. "Unless you don't want to be seen." A snicker. "Are you hiding something...or someone? Tch...tch...." He sounded just like an old lady.

"Nah, no such luck," Ron laughed. "There's just me."

Leisurely, Mick-Joe took a cigarette out of a badly scratched silver case. Still looking around, he offered Ron a smoke.

Ron sized up the cigarette before putting it between his lips. St. Pierre's finest. And highly illegal. Slimmer than the American brands too.

They lit up. Mick-Joe set his gun down and picked himself a comfortable spot.

Ron did the same. Man, these French smokes were strong. He coughed.

Mick-Joe didn't fool around. He got right to the point. "So, what are you doing hanging around with that Brook crowd?"

"Me?" Ron's voice was almost a squeak. Was Mick-Joe talking about Nicole?

"You and your buddies." Mick-Joe kicked off his rubber boots. He sneered. "They sure makes scarce when they sees me coming."

"Ah, they're okay."

"What do you mean, okay? Whose side are you on, buddy?" Mick-Joe shook his head in disgust. "They're Company scum. Their fathers are scum and that makes them scum too. Do you think there's any of them not on the same side as the Company? Ask them." He looked at Ron hard. "Ask them." He flicked the butt into the water. "If you're not too chicken."

Elbows on his knees, Ron stared at his smoke. "I worked in there on the surface...."

Ron looked at Mick-Joe. He was in a chatty mood, was he?

Mick laughed his crazy loon laugh. "I only lasted three weeks. That puffed-up tub of lard, Tubinski, wanted me to fix his gate. I told him no bloody way, told him where to shove his gatepost." He laughed again, loonier this time. "He got me fired."

Ron grinned. Mick-Joe. Leave it to him.

Mick-Joe lit up another cigarette. "Nursing that, aren't you?"

They puffed in silence with Mick taking three or four drags to Ron's one. "Yeah, the Company boys are finding out what work is now."

"They're not doing everything, are they?"

"Nah, they can't. They don't know how."

"Won't the mine flood or something?"

Mick-Joe shrugged and took a long drag. "It might. It'll be their own fault if it does."

"Do you think they'll shut her down?"

Another shrug. "Maybe. Won't make much difference."

"Then there'll be no work at all."

"Don't be so stupid, man. We survived before them and we'll survive after them." Mick-Joe studied the growing ash on the tip of his cigarette. "Survive better maybe."

"How come?"

Mick shifted so he could lean against the rock. "You know something? My old man died from the mine. So did my uncles, three of them in fact. Who says we wouldn't be better off without them?"

"My old man is going to St. John's next week," Ron said. Even as he was mouthing the words he didn't know why he was telling Mick-Joe, of all people. Maybe it was because Mick seemed almost human, the way he was talking about his old man. Or maybe Ron just wanted to say something that Mick-Joe couldn't ridicule.

But Mick-Joe could, and did. He pulled on his rubber boots and sneered at Ron. "What for? To get out of going on the picket line?"

If Mick thought he was going to get a rise out of Ron he was mistaken. No sense trying to hide what his old man was. Everyone knew. Ron's voice was flat and hard, like the beach rocks under his feet. "To see the doctors. Have some tests."

Mick-Joe stood up. "Is that right? Your old man?" He shook his head. "Another one."

"Whaddaya mean?"

Mick-Joe picked up his rifle. "Old Syl went in a couple weeks ago. You know Syl Stacey. Church Lane Syl?"

Ron felt like the blood was draining out of him. Useless he was. Couldn't manage a nod. He knew Syl all right. A couple weeks ago. Jeez, that was around the time....

Mick-Joe was still talking. "He let them operate. That's the end. Once you have the operation, you're finished. They say he'll never come out of there." He hoisted his gun to his shoulder. "Watched his last game, that boy." He kicked Ron's foot. "You okay, buddy? You looks like you seen a ghost."

Worse. Ron saw himself. Laughing his head off with the boys. At old Syl.

"So your old man –"

Ron cut him off. "It's just some tests," Ron said. "Mostly it's that smoker's cough he's got." It wasn't like Syl. Not the same thing at all. Syl was so old he was probably one of the first to go underground, back in the old days Mr. Bennie talked about.

"Smoker's cough?" Mick-Joe scoffed.

"Yeah. Maybe they won't find anything."

Mick-Joe looked at him with a mixture of pity and scorn. "Yep. And maybe the fog won't come in tonight."

Ron looked out across the water. Serves you right, Tarrant. What did you expect? Sympathy from the likes of Mick-Joe?

10

GIRLS.
Were they all weird, or just the ones Ron knew?

This morning he had the friendliest kind of smile for Nicole, and she strolled right past him, laughing at some idiotic thing Bert said.

Then he was all set for Jackie to be cheesed off at him because he hadn't shown up to work on the report last evening. And what did her royal highness do? She actually talked to him in a civil voice. Not only that. She flashed him a bashful grin and said he'd better show up this evening, and on time. The blotches of pink in her cheeks told Ron she wasn't as sure of herself as she put on. Blushing like that, she was kind of cute.

Al explained things to Ron later. "She's hooked, man," he said, meaning Nicole. "It's that Tarrant charm." He slapped Ron on the back. "She just couldn't resist."

"Yeah, then how come she's not talking to me?"

Al let out a loud belch. He must have been saving it all afternoon. The nuns didn't approve of rude body noises, as they called them. "That's nothing, old buddy. She's just trying to reel you in."

"You think so?"

Al stopped in the middle of the lane and shook his head. "Didn't I hear her in school asking you if you were going to the game?"

Ron nodded.

"Well, when you didn't, she got mad. I wasn't there five minutes when she asked me where you were."

"What did you tell her?"

Straight-faced, Al replied. "I said you had something urgent to take care of, but you appointed me to take your place."

Ron couldn't help but laugh. "Thanks a lot."

He punched Al's shoulder as hard as he could. Al didn't even flinch.

"Make up your mind, man," Al said. "She's not going to wait around all summer. Not that one."

"Not my fault. If she won't talk, she won't talk. Nothing I can do about it."

Al shook his head. "You dumb sod." Laying a

hand on Ron's shoulder, he doled out his advice. "You have to go up to her, and you have to tell her how sorry you are that you couldn't make it, see? And come up with a good reason too."

"What good reason?"

Al was getting loud. "How the hell should I know? Lie your head off, man."

Ron laughed at Al's earnestness. This was turning out to be a lot of trouble.

Later that evening he neared Jackie's house and saw her sitting on the front step. He'd never seen her with her hair pulled back like that in a ponytail. She should do it for school sometimes.

"Shove over," he said, giving her an exaggerated push as he lowered his lanky frame to sit next to her.

She made room for him.

Before Ron knew what he was saying he was using the advice Al had given him for Nicole. "Sorry I didn't make it yesterday. I took off. Went to Blue Beach."

"Is that why you weren't at the ball game either?"

"How'd you know?"

"Donna phoned last night. She asked if we had worked on the report, and when I said you didn't show up, she told me you weren't at the game either."

"Oh." He paused. "You're not mad?" There. That wasn't so hard. Al would have been proud.

She shook her head and grinned. "Just don't let it happen again."

"Okay," he said. Their eyes met, and both turned away, embarrassed.

Jackie moved them to safer ground then. "How come you skipped anyway?"

Ron leaned back, his elbows on the step. A sigh. "I don't know. Sometimes all that strike talk gets to me. I don't think Perky has any business bringing it into the school." He looked at her. "You?"

Jackie nodded. "I know what you mean. But pretending there's nothing going on won't solve anything either. Might make things worse."

"How?"

"Well, then somebody throws it in your face when you least expect, and there's hard feelings."

He flicked a fly off his knee. "It's going to cause hard feelings anyway."

Jackie turned back her sweater cuff. "Like how?"

Ron was stuck for a minute. Then he said, "Well, your grandad has the miner's disease, so you're against the Company. And here Donna's mom works at the store, so all she's worried about is losing her job." He sucked in his breath. "Just like my old man."

"Yes, but me and Donna are still friends. She understands about Grandad, and I understand about her mom needing a job."

Ron picked at a hangnail. "I just don't think it does any good to bring that stuff up."

"You'd rather people just bottled it in? How do you think anyone is going to understand where somebody else is coming from if they don't open their mouths?"

"I don't know. I just wish things were like before."

"With the men dying of silicosis, one by one, and no one saying a word?"

Ron could feel her scrutiny. And it wasn't a comfortable feeling.

"Let them bring home their paltry pay, coughing and spitting blood all the way to the grocery store? Till there's no one left to bring home a paycheque?" Her look took him on. "Then maybe it'll be your turn to go down in the mine. All the older men will be dead. Is that what you want, Ron?"

Ron flinched. Jeez, she didn't have to get so riled up. "No, he said, "that's not what I want. And I won't be in the mines, for sure. I'm getting out of here."

"Oh, I suppose you're going to quit school and

go to Toronto too, are you, Ron?" she taunted.

"Better than this," he said stubbornly. Now she was mad at him again. Just when they were getting friendly.

She got to her feet. "You don't mean that," she said, her tone matter-of-fact. She kicked his foot. "Come on. Grandad should be up now."

"Is he okay?" Ron wanted to put things back on an even keel.

"Well, he didn't sleep much last night, so after supper he went in on the bed for a while."

"How come he can't sleep?"

Jackie shrugged. "Sometimes it's his breathing. You can hear him all over the house, trying to catch his breath. And sometimes he has pain, or bad coughing."

Bad coughing. It couldn't be any worse than Ron's old man. "Is he going to be okay?"

Impatiently Jackie brushed back a strand of hair that had escaped the ponytail. Ron knew it was he who irritated her, not the hair.

Hand on the doorknob, she lowered her voice. "No, he's not going to be okay, Ron. We're hoping he won't get any worse for a while. Mom puts on a brave front, but I know she thinks he won't last long."

Ron wanted to cover his ears. He didn't want to know this about Mr. Bennie. Or to have it in his mind every time he sat down with Mr. Bennie and Jackie. He stood, one foot on the top step, lead it was, wouldn't move an inch. Just like his mouth. Couldn't have said a word if he tried.

Jackie held the door open. "Well, are you coming in, or aren't you?"

Ron heard her grandfather's breathy voice. "Mind your manners there, girl."

"Aw, Grandad, waste good manners on him?" she teased.

Ron managed to reply, "Your grandad's right, Jacko."

Mr. Bennie ignored their sparring and spoke to Ron. "Grand evening out there."

"Finest kind, sir."

The old man settled himself into his recliner by the window. Jackie and Ron pulled up chairs next to him.

"Now where was I?" he mused. "Jackie, read me what you have so far."

Jackie turned back a few pages.

Man, she was neat. Ron was glad Mr. Bennie hadn't asked him. What a snarl his notes were. He didn't think any of the bits of paper had gotten lost though, just all over the place and tattered to boot.

Jackie skimmed her notes. "Well. We have... how the place got started...."

"Richard Clarke and those fellas," Ron blurted out. He darn near burst a button he was so proud of himself. It was lost on Jackie; she didn't even look up.

"Then we did how the fishing went bad...the tidal wave...."

Ron couldn't recall the fishing part, but he remembered the tidal wave. So far he hadn't found a thing Jackie had said. Must be there somewhere.

"And last day you told us about how hard the men worked in starting up the mine. She read on. "...second-hand machinery...unloaded it for free...used the open-cut, or open-pit method, even though it was against good mining practices. That's where we stopped."

Ron scribbled as fast as he could. He didn't think he had that last part. Leaning over the binder balanced on his knee, he kept Jackie from seeing his notes. Who did she think she was, his mother? "Why did they use, uh...that method, if it wasn't good mining?" He'd show her a thing or two. She wasn't the only one who could ask dumb questions.

Mr. Bennie leaned forward. Ron could hear him wheezing. The old man nodded his approval. "That's a good question, Skipper." He sipped from the cup of tea Jackie had set on the windowsill. "The reason they used open-pit mining, which was removing the top layer of ground to get to the spar, was because it was cheaper than sinking shafts, you see."

Ron nodded and jotted down a few key words. At least he hoped they would be key words once he started to figure this all out.

"Why was it cheaper, Grandad?"

They waited for him to catch his breath. It was slow going.

Mr. Bennie set his mug down. "It took money to sink shafts and drive drifts and raises, money they claimed they didn't have. On top of that, the overburden...."

"What's that, sir?"

"Overburden is just the surface rock, or close to the surface." Mr. Bennie leaned towards them, his hands spreading to show the size of the boulders. "One hundred per cent fluorspar it was. And they didn't have to drill or dynamite to get at it." He sat back and rested before he went on. "All that was needed was to crush and hand-pick it, the ore was such high quality."

Ron started a clean page. He'd show Jacko he could take notes as good as hers any day. Jeez, now he went and missed what Mr. Bennie had just said.

"Could you say that last part again, Mr.

Bennie? I missed it when I turned the page."

He knew she gave him a dirty look; he could feel it. He also ignored it. Was she jealous, or what? "You were saying about digging the ditch...."

Quick as a wink, Jackie slid a note onto Ron's binder. Now there was a switch. She was writing him notes. It was nothing to get excited about, however. Ron read: *We're supposed to be sharing this time. It's MY turn.*

Ron wrote back. *Say please.*

She tipped his binder. Sneaky little bugger.

"That's right," Mr. Bennie said. "After some time they talked about digging a ditch. That was to lessen the height the old pumps would have to pump the water, you see." He took a breathing spell before he went on. "The understanding was, if the ditch was unsuccessful, there would be no pay. And if it was, the men would get their regular fifteen cents an hour."

"So, was it?" Jackie asked.

Mr. Bennie nodded. "For a while it was. It was dug in February in the worst kind of weather. Heavy drifts and frost. And the men finally got their wages."

Ron sat up straight. "Man, you couldn't pay me enough to do work like that."

Mr. Bennie gazed out the window. "Thanks to

these men, young fellow, and the others who came after them, men like your father, you won't have to."

Mrs. Haskell spoke from the kitchen door. "Here's a fresh cup of tea, Dad. They're not tiring you out now, are they?" She picked up the empty cup and set the other down, her eyes searching her father's face.

"I'm fine, dear. Talking to these young ones is the highlight of my day."

Jackie's mother smiled. "Just so you don't overdo it."

"Mr. Bennie, what do you think of the strike? Do you agree with it?" Waiting for the answer, Ron felt tense.

Mr. Bennie pulled himself up straighter in the chair. "Well, son, sometimes a strike's the only way." There was a spark in his eye and fire in his voice. "Over the years the Union tried everything under the sun to make the Company listen." He broke out in a sweat and sank back against the headrest. "I'm not at the table this time, but I'm sure 'tis no different."

"I told you Grandad was a Union man," Jackie said with pride.

Ron looked at the old man, fighting for every breath. He would have loved to have been able to see him in his day, standing up to the Company.

Fighting for the miners. Curious, he asked, "Does the Union go as far back as the start-up of the mines?"

Mr. Bennie rubbed his forehead as he thought back. "The first Union formed in 1937. Membership grew fast. There were lots of issues. Wages way too low for the type of work, and the dreadful conditions." He wheezed and patted his face with his hanky. "Small wonder so many are falling victim to the dust."

Jackie doodled on her book.

Ron didn't get it. "But Mr. Bennie," he said, with a tilt of his head, "if it was open pit, how come there was so much dust?" The wind and weather around here should have taken care of it pretty fast.

Mr. Bennie changed position in the chair. "No, no. The dust and smoke problems didn't start up in earnest until the first shaft was sunk."

"Why did they change from the open pit?" Jackie asked.

"Well, when Black Duck reached seventy feet, the old second-hand pumps couldn't handle the water. So a shaft was sunk, and drifting began." Mr. Bennie looked at them. "A drift is like a horizontal passageway. In the drifts and stopes the drilling was done with what they called a dry hammer."

They both nodded.

After a little spell, Mr. Bennie continued. "I minds working a whole shift, the hammer slung on my shoulder with the drill hole practically next to my mouth. Times I'd use curtain screen or a piece of cheesecloth, whatever I had, over my mouth to keep out the dust. In seconds it would be clogged...mere seconds." He shook his head, as if appalled at the memory. "And every few minutes I'd have to shut off the machine to clear the dust out of my eyes and nose." Mr. Bennie grimaced and closed his eyes. "And the further the drifts advanced, the worse the dust and smoke got."

"Wasn't there someone to monitor things like that?" Ron asked.

Mr. Bennie's tired, indulgent smile included them both. "Nothing like that till years later. Years later. Sure, in those days there was no such thing as miners safety boots...or skull guards...or the safety lamps they have nowadays." He tried for a more comfortable position.

Jackie picked up the cushion that had fallen on the floor and tucked it behind his back.

"We used carbide lamps. And when a fellow ran out of carbide, he used a candle stuck in a can." Mr. Bennie leaned back for a rest. "And the black spittle we coughed up with them carbide lamps. As black as squid ink it was." He smiled weakly and stared out the window. "The cracks the men used to make about that."

Jackie tapped her pen on her notebook. "It was a good thing the Union came along."

Mr. Bennie nodded. "The Company didn't like the idea too much, as you can imagine. Between March and December of 1941, there were five strikes. They were lively times, I tell you."

"So, what happened, Grandad?"

"After a spell the government appointed a Dispute Board. They looked at the state of the air in the mines. Their report said there was no trace of foul air." Mr. Bennie's voice was flat. "They didn't find anything because there was no drilling or blasting for days before their visit." The old man rubbed the knuckles of his left hand. "So nothing was done as far as ventilation was concerned." His tone was full of regret. "Maybe if there had been, there wouldn't be so many men going to their graves before their time."

Ron opened his mouth and closed it. Twice. But then he just couldn't leave it alone. "So you would think, wouldn't you, that all the miners at least, would support the strike? It's for their benefit, right?"

"Most do, most do," Mr. Bennie replied in a tired voice.

"Not Dad. He's dead set against it." There, he'd said it and he was glad.

There was a long pause. The old man was so quiet Ron got worried. He looked at Jackie.

"Grandad?" she said, her voice tentative.

With an effort, Mr. Bennie straightened himself in the chair. He fought for breath. "I've known your dad a long time. He's a good worker, a good miner. One of the best. If he don't agree with the strike, I'm sure he has his reasons and they're good ones." He looked intently at Ron. "Did you ask him?"

Jackie gave Ron a pointed look. "Yeah, Ron. Why don't you ask your dad?"

Ron snorted. Now wouldn't that be a picture. As if he could just go home and sit down with the old man and have a conversation about the strike. Ask him. He tried to laugh, but it didn't come off. "Some chance of that. He won't even talk to me. And now he's worse since he found out he's got to go to St. John's." Ron clamped his mouth shut. He should just sew his trap up and be done with it.

Mr. Bennie nodded. He looked like he was all in.

Jackie stood up. "That's enough for this evening, Grandad." She muttered to Ron, "I'll meet you outside." She practically shoved him out the door.

Fine. He could take a hint. But he wasn't waiting outside. He understood her not wanting to upset her grandfather. He hadn't meant to. It had just slipped out. But she needn't think she was going to bawl him out about it.

Halfway across the field, he heard her calling him. He turned around. She jogged towards him, shrugging her arms into her jacket. "Wait up."

He waited. If she started on him, he'd take off.

"Let's go sit on the graveyard steps and talk," she said, buttoning up.

"The boneyard steps?"

She laughed. "Why not? No one there to gossip."

"About being seen with me?" He didn't think he liked that.

She slapped at his arm. "God, you're dense. I meant no one can hear what we're yapping about. Get it?"

"Oh, okay." Dense, she said he was.

They jumped the brook and crossed the road to the wide concrete steps. She was right. This was a nice quiet place, except for the occasional car coming over the hill into town or going in around the bottom of the harbour.

They settled themselves on the step before she asked, "What's this about your dad? I didn't know he was sick."

Ron studied his sneakers. "I didn't mean to upset your grandfather. It just came out."

"I know."

The kindness in her voice was unexpected. But nice.

Ron grinned sheepishly. "So you didn't come after me to bawl me out?"

"No, I wanted to talk. I know you're good at that." She was laughing at him again. He didn't know what to say then. Or again in the next minute when a brown station wagon sailed by. The Brook crowd were packed in like sardines and Nicole's face was plastered in the window, wide-eyed and open-mouthed.

Ron slumped. Yep. Just his luck.

"There goes your girlfriend," Jackie announced with too much delight for Ron's liking.

He tossed a loose piece of cement across the road. "She's not my girlfriend." He didn't know what Jacko found so hilarious.

"You're blushing, Ronnie!" Still laughing, Jackie waggled her finger in his face.

He grabbed for it, but she was too quick.

Her eyes followed the station wagon in around The Bottom. "She says she is."

11

RON TOOK ADVANTAGE OF HIS FATHER BEING gone. He was down on the picket line every chance he got. No one to get off the head with him about it.

Except Tuesday night.

He had turned into the yard at a run. His mother, fist raised, was in the window waiting for him. He'd expected she would be. As soon as it got dark she started worrying, and praying. By now she'd have him lying out in the hospital. Ron wished the place was half as lively as her imagination had it.

He wasn't too worried. He couldn't remember her ever going beyond making the fist. The old man now, that was a different story.

She settled down once Ron told her where he'd been. They sat back with a cup of tea, just the two of them. He told her the latest news. "They're saying that the *Hamildoc* won't be around much longer."

"Is that so?" She sat sideways in his father's

place at the table, one arm across her middle, the other hand holding her cup. She could've been drinking muddy water and not known it, she was that distracted looking. Had the old man on her mind most likely. You'd think she'd be glad to get a break from him.

"The Company was losing too much money with the ore boat just sitting there day after day."

She nodded. Ron just about choked on his tea when she said, "Serves them right. It's about time someone stood up to them."

Man, he was proud of her.

The next evening after supper he looked his mother straight in the face and assured her he'd finished off his homework in school. It wasn't exactly the truth. He'd get caught up on the work tomorrow, courtesy of Duck's notebook.

Ron headed down the harbour.

He and Jackie hadn't worked on the report for a few days. Mr. Bennie wasn't feeling up to it.

Ron didn't mind going in there any more. Mr. Bennie was all right. He knew his stuff, and he could tell some good yarns too.

No, he didn't mind going at all. At first it had been a laugh bugging Jackie. He still liked to bug her. But now he liked talking with her too. Serious stuff, as well as fooling around. Today at the end of break he'd been surprised to see her

140

hanging around outside the classroom door. He'd been even more surprised when he'd realized she was waiting for him. She told Ron her grandad wasn't well enough again today to meet with them. Ron was kind of disappointed. He thought, by the way she said it, that maybe Jackie was too. She'd teased him that he could use the time to try and decipher his notes.

Now Ron broke into a run. Bert and Al were already there, down the hill towards the land-wash, passing the time by seeing how far they could spit. In between gobs they speculated on when the boat would haul anchor.

"Could be tonight if the fog holds off like she is now," said Bert.

"Nah. Early in the morning, I'd say. Being the size she is, she won't take any chances." Al, stretched out on the grass, looked up at Ron. "Whaddaya say, Ron? Give us your best educated guess there, old buddy."

Ron shrugged and sat down. "Dunno. I'd like to be here though."

Al leaned back on his elbow. He craned his neck to see up the hill. With that he let out an unmerciful roar – Al's throat could outdo the foghorn any day – and rolled over on his front. "Hey...hey Jacko, come down here!"

Ron's head jerked around so fast a bone

cracked in his neck.

Yep. There she was. She hove up her hand to them, then turned her back and joined a bunch of women on lawn chairs.

"Who's that she's with?" asked Bert.

"Her sister, the one that's married to Bill... ah...whatshisname, from up the shore," said Al.

"Lamb," contributed Ron.

Al squinted up at him and shoved his Buddy Holly glasses up on his nose. "Know a lot about her, don't ya, Skipper?"

Al was a pain. Ron tried to weasel out of it. "They live just over the road in that new house behind Aunt Bessy's."

"Yeah, yeah, sure."

Bert looked from one to the other. "What's going on?"

Al worked up a serious look. "Not for me to say, old man." A pause. He bobbed his head at Ron. "Ask loverboy here. He's the one spending his evenings at the Haskell house."

Ron was on Al before he got the last word out. He gave Al's skull a good knuckle rub before Al could throw him off.

Bert was insulted, or acted like he was. With Bert it was hard to tell. "How come nobody told me?"

Al, a dirty grin on his face, straightened his glasses and smoothed his hair.

Ron's fist was up, threatening to have another go at him if he as much as opened his mouth.

Al laughed, and open the mouth he did. Ron let fly with his fist, using Al's arm as a punching bag.

Shielding himself from Ron's punches, and laughing at the same time, Al filled Bert in. "Ron, old loverboy here...ouch...is doing the research paper with Jackie." A yelp of pain. "In there every evening." A louder yelp. "Okay, okay, I won't say another word."

"Must be an awful big secret," added Bert.

Ron knew he was sixteen shades of red; he felt every one of them, and more besides. He hoped to God Jackie hadn't heard, that she would stay put up there with her sister.

Ron wished he could escape. No chance. They'd only call after him and the whole hill would hear about it.

"What's the big secret, eh Ron?" Al goaded. "How come you didn't tell us?"

Ron grabbed him just above the knee and used his thumb and finger to put the squeeze on.

Al shoved at Ron, calling up the hill, "Jackie, come call him off." Through big ha-ha laughs he hollered, "He says he'll only listen to you."

Jackie would never speak to him again after this. Did she hear them? She'd have to be deaf not to.

Bert saved Ron. Bert noticed his father in the

midst of a bunch of men standing by the side of the road. "Let's go see what's up."

Ron, for one, was glad to go.

AL WAS RIGHT. THE *HAMILDOC* DID LEAVE IN THE early morning hours. Not a sign of her by the time Ron went to school.

Bert was all smiles when he told them about it. He said she snuck away before dawn. Not one ounce of spar aboard her.

Ron was glad about the spar. But he was disappointed he hadn't seen her leaving. Would have been nice to be able to curse her out of the harbour. Too bad.

Ron steered clear of Jackie during the day. He didn't know how to tackle explaining about the racket Al kicked up last evening. What if he started and she didn't know what he was talking about? Some fool he'd seem then. Or what if she had heard it all and was mad? He was better off to make himself scarce.

A little while after supper, Jackie phoned. It was the first time she'd ever phoned him. And it was Ron's rotten luck to have Wayne answer. "You want Ron?" Wayne snickered into the receiver. "Just a minute now."

Ron grabbed for it, but his wiry little brother

slipped the receiver behind his back and danced out of Ron's reach. "Hey, Mom," Wayne called loudly, "is Ron allowed to talk to girls on the phone?"

Ron's shove sent Wayne sprawling and got the phone away from him but gave Ron no satisfaction. He had to talk to Jackie with that idiot crowing in the background. No wonder he didn't have much to say on the phone.

Jackie told him relatives from up the shore had come to visit her grandfather, so they couldn't meet this evening either.

"Fine," he mumbled. She said something about maybe tomorrow. Ron said okay. He didn't want to give Wayne any more ammunition. Besides, maybe Jackie was making excuses. After last evening she probably didn't want him around. At least she could have come right out and said it. He kicked the cupboard door.

He wasn't off the phone when Wayne started. "Ron, let's go out and take shots. You can be in goal first."

"Not now," Ron snapped.

"When? You said you would."

Ron hated it when Wayne got whiny. "Some other time." Right now he could easily drop his brother at the garbage dump with the bears and leave without a look back.

He needled Wayne about his team losing their soccer game to Lawn. "Anybody who can't beat the Lawners, now that's some sad, that is. I call that pitiful."

Wayne pouted into his Archie comic. "Not as pitiful as your face."

Ron yanked the comic out of his brother's hand. Wayne started yelling, which brought their mother. The place was in an uproar and according to Mom it was all Ron's fault.

"Here," she said, snatching a book off the daybed. "Read this to Carrie before she goes to bed."

Ron had read books to Carrie hundreds of times, before she was sent off to bed, but tonight he couldn't limit himself to the words on the page. He called Peter Rabbit old Big Ears and changed the story so much Carrie was fit to be tied.

She grabbed the book from him, took it to her mom, and declared Ron was never going to read her another story. He couldn't help but grin at how cute she looked scowling across the kitchen at him.

"What's the matter with you tonight?" his mother asked Ron, as Carrie crawled onto her lap.

"I want to go walk the picket line."

"Sure, the boat's gone. There's no one there."

"Not that one. The one in the Brook. With the men."

"Ron, stop talking nonsense." She tut-tutted.

"That's for the miners, not the likes of you."

"Bert goes with his dad."

She sniffed. "I'm sure Bert's mom won't let him miss school to walk the picket line."

"He goes after school and on weekends."

Silence for a bit. Then she said, "Well, your dad's not here, is he?"

"Wouldn't matter anyhow. He wouldn't let me go if he was here."

She brushed Carrie's hair off her forehead and said nothing.

"So why can't I go with Bert?"

"No, Ron, your father's tormented enough already. I don't want you making it any worse."

"How's my going on the picket line going to make him worse? He won't even know."

"Now, how do you think you're going to keep that from him?"

"So what if he finds out? Why should he care anyhow? He doesn't about anything else."

"Is that what you thinks?"

"All he does is swear and be miserable."

"Ron, don't be talking such foolishness. You knows he cares. Why do you think he gets so upset with you about school?" She didn't wait for a reply, which was a good thing because she wouldn't have liked hearing what Ron was thinking. "It's because he wants a better life for you

147

than he had. And you just throw it all away, scraping by, doing as little as possible. How many times has he said to me, 'I wish I'd had his chances'?"

Ron just sat there on the daybed and took it. His mother had never bawled him out like this before. He'd expect it from the old man, but not from her.

And she wasn't finished. "Who do you think puts food on the table?" She was wound right up now. On and on she went.

"Yeah, Ron." Carrie was glad he was getting heck.

"Well, he doesn't have to be so damn nasty about it."

"You watch your language now." His mother's tone was sharp. Then she sighed. "God only knows he's hard to live with. But he's not all bad. There's a lot of good there too."

Ron grunted. It must be buried awful deep then, because he sure couldn't see it. And that grunt. Freaked him out. What if he had inherited it from the old man? Could grunting be inherited? Man, he'd hang himself if it could. Mom nudged Carrie off her knee. "Time for bed."

"It's not even dark yet," Carrie protested.

"It's not dark till late now, but you still have to get up for school. You can read for a little bit."

Carrie was satisfied.

As she passed Ron, she tossed her curls and deliberately turned away from him. It was just too tempting. Ron scooped her up, swung her around till she shrieked with delight, and planted noisy wet slobbers on her chubby little cheeks.

"Ron, don't!" Mom said. "You'll get her all worked up, and she won't be able to sleep."

Ron let Carrie go then and she ran off, daring him to chase her.

After a second fat slice of bread and bakeapple jam, Ron too went up to bed. He looked across to the harbour, lathered in fog right up tight to the causeway. He liked the look of it. The puny lights of the two poles lit up nothing but the fog itself, thick and grey as the sheep's wool his mother used to knit the old man's work socks.

Yes, sir. Ron was going with Bert. No one, or nothing, was going to stop him. Tomorrow after school he'd cut across the meadow behind the liquor store and Batten's Hill. That way he wouldn't have to pass by his house. He'd go to the Union Office on the top road and see if the shifts were posted. He'd tell whoever was there that he was taking his old man's place while he was gone to St. John's. He couldn't see why anyone would argue with that.

As it turned out, he didn't need to. Bert's father

stopped as Ron and Bert walked down the lane from school the next evening. "Get in," Bert said, hopping in the front.

Ron opened the car door. Behind him he heard, "Hey, Ron, where're you going?"

One foot in, he said to Wayne, "Tell Mom I'm going to the softball game."

"What game? There's no game, is there?"

Ron ignored his nosy brother and slammed the door.

They drove in around The Bottom and out the top road to the Union Hall, a one-room clapboard building set back fifty feet or so from the road.

Careful to stay behind Bert and his dad, Ron sauntered up to the uneven front steps, taking his cue from Bert, and trying to act as if coming here to the Union Hall was no big deal. Except that it was. This was where the action was, where the strike plans were made, and the decisions about what offers and counter-offers to make to the Company.

Ron wiped the back of his hand across his mouth; no stupid grins, this was serious stuff.

Though from the looks of it, the fellows inside didn't seem to think so. There were a half-dozen or so of them, all laughing their heads off. Big Lar stopped midsentence and nodded to Bert's dad. He was tilted back dangerously far on the chrome office chair. "...After that we never had any more trouble with him on night shift." More laughs. Ron's eyes were on the chair. He half expected it to buckle any second under Lar's considerable bulk.

"Who're you talking about? Weisner?" Bert's dad asked, grinning as he lit up an Export A.

Bud Lockyer, leaning on the windowsill, nodded. "I wouldn't ask my dog to work for him, scumbag. He didn't last long, did he?"

"Is that the new schedule?" asked Bert's dad, going over to the far wall.

Isaac Beck got up from the garbage pail he'd been sitting on and righted it. "We didn't put Leo on this time, until we find out what's happening with him."

Ron stood there, powerless to stop the rush of red to his face. He felt sick, wondering what they were going to say next about his old man, what they were thinking. They did know who Ron was, didn't they? Yeah, Bud knew him, and so did Ern over by the window. Sure to God, they wouldn't say stuff right in front of him.

Ron raked his fingers over his hair. His hands trembled. Nerves. He jammed his fists in his pockets to keep them still. "I can go on for him...on the picket," he blurted out. "For Leo...for my dad," he corrected himself, in case someone there didn't know who he was.

They were looking at him now. Oh, God. What was he doing? Dying on his feet, that's what. He couldn't breathe. He couldn't get his thoughts straight. It had all seemed easy enough last night when he was deciding what to do. His gaze jumped around to all of them. He didn't know who he should be talking to. "He wants me to." He blundered on. "He said before he left. I was going to come up today anyway...." He ran out of breath and gulped for air. "To tell you, I mean to ask if it's okay."

Big Lar eased the chair back to all fours. There was a creak, a relieved thank you probably from the chair. "You sure your dad won't mind, son?"

Ron shook his head, too fast, too much. "Not a chance." Like an eager kid. He was disgusting himself even. He looked at Bert. But Bert was at his father's elbow studying the schedule. He didn't seem to be paying any attention to Ron.

Bert's father was listening though. "He can come with me and Bert. I'll talk to Leo when he gets back."

That settled it then. Ron breathed easier. He would get to go, on the weekend.

No matter what.

12

THE TRUCK WAS IN THE YARD WHEN RON GOT home from school Wednesday.

He's back, just like the cat.

"Thought he was a goner, but the cat came back..." Ron bleated. It was a passable imitation of Belle Island's Harry Hibbs, if Ron did say so himself.

Ron might be a goner when the old man found out about his going on the picket line Friday night. Didn't matter. He was going anyway. Ron started up again. *"Thought he was a goner –"*

His mother met him in the doorway, a frown on her face. "Stop that racket. Your father's asleep."

Ron could see that. There was Himself, stretched out on the kitchen daybed. The snores out of him would wake the dead. And Mom accused *him* of making a racket.

Not big on goodbye and hello stuff, his old man. Slept right through it. He'd left for St. John's in the middle of the morning when they were all in school. Showed up in the middle of the day again when they were all in school. A bit of a pattern here, Ron figured.

He slapped his books down on the counter before checking out the fridge. Good and loud, he asked, "When did Dad get home?"

"Around two o'clock," his mother answered in a near whisper. "And you lower your voice."

Ron ignored her black look and hacked off a hunk of cheese.

She got after Wayne and Carrie too. She nearly bit their heads off when all they asked was whether their father had brought them presents from St. John's. Then Carrie sidled over to the suitcase. Wayne wasn't having Carrie get her paws on any presents meant for him. An argument started. Their mother packed them both off outdoors.

Ron was poisoned with her. He wasn't about to start whispering. No way was he going to act like the place was a funeral parlour just because the old man was snoozing. He was probably sleeping off the beer anyway.

"What's for supper?" he asked, as loud and brash as he dared. He eyed the dried cod and the pile of cooked potatoes on the counter. His mother was cutting up onions.

"Fishcakes."

"Good." Something decent at least.

The fishcakes turned out to be the only decent thing about supper. The old man slept all through it, if you could call it that. Every snore and snort trailed off in a rattle or a wheeze. Some background music, that was. The young ones hardly opened their mouths except to shovel in a forkful. Mom was no better. She was off in some tortured place, if her face was anything to go by. Ron shut up and ate too. He wondered about the tests. Did Mom know something? Was that why she was so crabby?

They were almost done when the old man roused himself. The rattling finally worked up to a full-blown hacking that got him up. Bent double in a spasm of coughing, he veered past them to the bathroom.

The fancy St. John's doctors didn't do anything for that cough, did they? Probably no medicine potent enough to touch it. It would have to be awful strong stuff to clear up that much nicotine – two packs a day. His father would have to give up smoking altogether. Fat chance.

Ron wiped his plate with a crust of bread and stuffed it in his mouth. "That was good, Mom."

He went to the counter and brought the cake tin to the table, keeping it to himself.

Wayne's mouth worked its way around a mound of mashed potato and fish. "Mom, what's he got there?" he asked.

"Now Ron, why didn't you wait with that?"

Wayne's skinny arm snaked out, but Ron was too quick. He teased, "Finish your supper first, children, and if there's any left...." Ron pried off the lid and looked over the date squares, finally settling on the biggest one he could find.

"Mom, make him save me one," Carrie whined. "I don't like this fish – it got too many bones."

"You won't find any bones in that, Carrie. I took them all out. Now eat up, and then you can have a date square."

Carrie glared at Ron. "Don't you eat them all." She had shredded her fishcake. "There are bones too. See that?" She'd found the bones all right and lined them up on the edge of her plate. Three puny little things so small you'd need a magnifying glass for a good look at them.

When Ron reached for a second square and devoured it in two bites, Wayne went right off the head. Rising from his chair, he grabbed for the tin and nearly upset it.

Their mother took over then. "Ron, that's

enough. Save some for somebody else. They're your father's favourites. At least let him have one before you devour them all." She set some squares out on a plate.

Dad stood behind her. "It's all right, Sadie."

Ron stopped in mid-chew. Had anyone else heard that? He looked around the table. Guess not. Except for him, the rhythm of chewing had not been broken. Just what had them St. John's doctors done? Drained the nasty fluid out of him?

He looked at his father. They must have done something, because he looked different. Hard to say in what way. Almost like the fight was gone out of him. Ron shrugged off his uneasiness. Whatever it was, he was sure it was only temporary. Until the "favourite" son restored the old man to his old miserable self.

Perhaps it was the beer. Probably had to do without it the past couple weeks. Ron couldn't imagine the hospital serving up Blue Star. Maybe the beer had kept him puffed up and without it he looked deflated.

The old man took off to the front room and came back with a brown paper bag. He dumped it in the middle of the table. Out came three fat, foot-long pencils, blue, they were. And small red and yellow coil notepads, a pair of rosary beads (rosary beads for God's sake!), and a pen that had five or six refills of different colours.

You'd think these two had never seen anything store-bought in their lives, the way they carried on. What a fuss. Carrie and Wayne grabbed the same pencil and would have socked each other, had their father not tossed another one at them. Then Wayne got rory-eyed because Carrie took a red notebook just like his.

Ron recognized the picture of Cabot Tower stamped on everything. Underneath was written *Souvenir of Signal Hill.* Except the rosary beads.

"Say thank you to your dad."

Carrie stood up on her chair. "Thank you, Daddy dear," she said, with a smack on his cheek.

Wayne grinned and started a pencil sword fight with his sister. "Thanks, Dad."

The old man picked up the rosary. The beads draped over his stained fingers with their yellowed nails. It was almost sacrilegious. "You know Aunt Martha's daughter, the nun? She came to see me."

His wife nodded. "Sr. Florence. I saw Sister Martha at Mass last Sunday. She asked what hospital you were in."

"She left me the beads. I told her I wasn't much for praying." An understatement, Ron figured, if ever there was one. "She laughed and said I could pass them on to you."

Mom took the beads, kissed the cross, and blessed herself.

Ron helped himself to another square. No one squawked. They were too wrapped up in their souvenirs. The table was empty but for one over-sized pencil and the pen.

He felt the old man's look. "What's the matter? Stuff not good enough for you?"

Ron licked a crumb off the side of his mouth. Pens and pencils didn't exactly give him a rush, he had to admit. Just to keep the peace he picked up the pen. His old man's eyes were still on him. "I'll have this one."

A nod. "For all that writing you do."

What kind of a comment was that? Good God. He wasn't trying to make a joke, was he?

Carrie saw her chance to get the other pencil. "Can I have that, if Ron's not taking it?"

"I'll have it," said Wayne, reaching across the table. "You'll only give it to that bowlegged Lisa."

"Neither one of you is having it." Ron tossed the pencil in the air like a drumstick. It spun around and he caught it.

HE STUCK THE PENCIL IN HIS BACK POCKET WHEN he went to Jackie's place later that evening.

Jackie answered his tap on the partly-open

porch door. "Hi, come in," she said. The meter man would have got more enthusiasm. He wondered what was up.

She led him into the kitchen, where her books were already spread out on the table. He hadn't done anything to make her mad, had he?

It was awful quiet in here. Don't say they all went and left him alone here with Jacko. Nah. Mr. Bennie must be here.

She perched on the chair, one leg under her, chin in hand. The picture of dejection, she was. A cute picture though.

Binder still under his arm, Ron sat down too. His knee grazing the chrome leg of the table made him aware that his leg was jiggling and he stopped. Something was not right, whatever it was.

"Grandad's in the hospital." There was fear in Jackie's voice.

"Aw, Jeez..." He reached out to her, pure instinct, then realized what he was doing and stopped himself. The hand was adrift on her open notebook, and he couldn't for the life of him haul it back. "What happened? When?" His own voice was none too robust.

She joined her hands in front of her, interlocking her fingers, and rubbed one thumb on the other. "This afternoon, while I was in school.

He wasn't very good this morning, having a hard time breathing. Then, Mom said, he got worse around one o'clock, and they took him in."

She was going to have the skin rubbed off that thumb if she didn't slack off. Ron slid the binder onto the table. Then he gripped both her hands in his and pulled her to her feet. "C'mon, let's go for a walk. Clear your head."

She hesitated on their way out. "I wonder if I should lock the door? Mom's at the hospital. She and my sister. They won't be back for a while yet."

While Jackie hunted in the drawer for the house key, Ron slid the pencil out of his back pocket and hid it under the books on the table.

They jumped the brook and took the road to Salmon Hole, past the cemetery and a clearing where a half-dozen or so rusted-out cars had been dumped. After a while Ron said, "If your grandad's going to be in the hospital for a bit, I wouldn't mind going to see him, if he's up to it."

"Sure. He'd be glad to see you."

"Do you think we could, ah, go see him..." He was trying to find the right words, words that wouldn't sound like he was moving in on her. "...sometime if you're going, let me know, and I'll come along?"

"Sure."

He breathed easier. She hadn't hesitated at all.

They walked in companionable silence. When the stink of the garbage dump reached their noses, they turned back. "Let's run," Jackie said.

"Run or race?"

"Well, I hope you won't be embarrassed having to eat my dust." And she took off.

He caught up to her and they ran, skidding on the loose gravel, till the road began to slope down to the cemetery.

When they'd caught their breath, Jackie said, "We might have to finish our reports without Grandad."

"Yeah?" He'd thought of that. Wouldn't be so low as to bring it up at a time like this. But now that Jackie had, it was okay. Ron was careful with his words. "Due pretty soon, isn't it? Next week, or the week after?"

"Next Thursday."

Okay for her. She knew it all. Ron took aim and kicked a rock into the bushes. He'd never be able to make sense of that mess he had in his binder. Not by himself. He should never have started this. And Mr. Bennie expected a copy too. Maybe if he stayed sick it wouldn't matter. God, he was rotten. He hadn't meant that.

They jumped the brook. His foot went in. He felt the water seep in through his sneaker and swore.

Jackie looked at him, but said nothing.

"I'll come in and pick up my binder," he said, aware of his gruff tone.

She raised her eyebrows at him. "Aren't you gonna stay and do some work?"

He supposed he was, if she put it like that.

"Or have you got it all figured out now, and you don't need me or Grandad anymore?"

A slow grin took over his face. "I guess I could stay and help you out a bit, if you ask nice."

"That'll be the day," she said, and stamped on his toe, the wet one. Did she mean that'll be the day when he was smart enough to be helping her? Or did she mean...heck, he didn't care what she meant. He was staying.

Once inside, Jackie was all business. Pen in hand, she reached for her notebook. "We have to decide exactly what we're gonna do."

Ron opened his binder and sluffed through until he found his notes. "You mean you don't know either? Now I don't feel so bad."

"Oh yeah, Ron. I'm sure you've been staying up nights worrying about this." She didn't even give him a chance to show his hurt feelings. "I was thinking that I could do how the miners started to get sick and all that, and how they started to put pressure on the government. And bring that right up to the present."

She looked so intense. He nodded. "Sounds good."

"I suppose you haven't got a pen again, have you?"

She shook her head at him and moved to get up to look for one.

He'd forgotten all about the fat pencil. He whipped it out from under the books and doodled her name. "I have too."

The look of surprise on her face! And the laugh! Ron wouldn't have missed it for anything. And he was the cause of it. A comedian is what he should be.

Still laughing, Jackie grabbed the pencil from him. "Where did you get this?"

"Dad brought it. He's back from St. John's."

She was serious now. "How is he?"

Ron shrugged. "Okay, I guess." He knew, as he was saying the words, that he didn't believe them himself.

Jackie seemed to be waiting for him to say more. But Ron didn't want to think about, let alone explain, that niggling feeling he had about his father.

Finally Jackie said, "I hope he's gonna be okay."

"Yeah."

"About the report," she said, "did you have anything in mind to do?"

"I don't know." He didn't have a clue. "Maybe something about the strikes...."

She nodded. "Good idea. And if you worked in about the start-up of the Union and how the men began to organize, you'd have enough material, I think."

Ron nodded, as if that was what he'd been planning all along.

There were footsteps in the porch.

"How's Grandad?" Jackie asked her mother in the doorway.

"About the same," sighed Mrs. Haskell. "Hello, dear," she greeted Ron.

Jackie put the kettle on to make her mom a cup of tea.

Ron closed his binder.

"Tomorrow night we'll go through the notes and mark off the ones we each can use."

He nodded. Sounded good to him.

Mrs. Haskell disappeared into the front room with her purse.

"Don't forget your pencil," Jackie said, eyeing it on the table.

"Aw, you hold on to it. You're dying to have it, I can tell."

She grinned at him. "Get out of here. You're cracked, you are."

He grinned back. "G'night, Jacko."

The truck was in the yard when he got home. Either the old man hadn't gone to the Stella Maris for a beer, or he'd had an early night of it. Either way would be a miracle. For sure he would have picked up a dozen. No miracle strong enough to put a stop to that.

The porch door was ajar. Ron kicked off his sneakers on the mat. He reached for the knob. Paused when he heard their voices. Must have been the tone that made his ears prick up and listen. It didn't sound like his father ranting on in his usual way about God knows what. And they weren't arguing.

His father's voice. "You're going to have some trouble with him when I'm gone."

Some trouble with who?

His mother then. "Now, Leo, don't worry about Ron. He's a good boy."

They had no business talking about him when he wasn't there. Ron held his breath in case he'd miss a word.

"How are you going to get him to finish school if I'm not around? He's as lazy as...as...Uncle Greg's cat."

Uncle Greg's cat. Right. What was the old man going on about?

"Leo, he's not going to quit school. He'll show more interest when he grows up a bit."

Ron bristled. Grows up a bit, yeah.

"Yes, but I mightn't be around when he decides he's ready to grow up, I tell you. The doctors are only giving me a year, or two at the most."

Silence. A long one.

Ron's insides seized up. A year or two?

13

THIRD PERIOD.

Perky reminded the class that their reports were due in exactly one week. Then she tossed another one of her brilliant ideas at them. "I was thinking...." She paused.

Groans all around.

"I think it would be a good idea to have you present your reports orally...so everyone can benefit from your research."

Silence, right down to the last girl.

Perky surveyed the room, a half smile on her face. "Here's what I'll do to make it more appealing to you." She perched on the edge of the desk and adjusted her garb. "I'll read and grade your papers first. But then I'll give bonus points for an oral presentation." She folded her arms, delighted with herself.

Ron sighed. There was Marlene, the arm waving like an old sock on the clothesline. "You mean extra points, Sister? On top of our mark?"

"Exactly."

Nods and smiles.

Ron was disgusted. They were pitiful, taken in like that for a few measly marks. Perky must be smirking right up her nun sleeve.

There were some who weren't impressed by her bonus points. Duck was one of them. He looked across at Ron. "I'm satisfied with my mark. You?"

Ron nodded. Good old Duck. You could always count on him. Ron would be satisfied with his mark too, whatever it turned out to be.

He looked across at Jackie. From this angle he could see her sitting, chin in hand. Her hair fell over her face. He smiled inside. He knew that any second she would tuck it behind her ear. Yep. There she went. No sign of a nod, or a smile, on her face. Ron was grateful for that. Glad that she wasn't taken in by Perky either. In fact, judging by the set of her jaw, Jackie might be just as fed up with this nun as Ron was. Maybe she was beginning to see that Ron was right about Sister Pat poking her nose where it didn't belong.

When Jackie grabbed his sleeve on the way out at lunchtime Ron was mildly surprised.

"I have to talk to you," she said.

Whatever it was, Ron knew her mind was

already made up. And he didn't like the look of it. "What's up?"

Jackie steered him away from the flow of kids leaving the building. "I think we should do the report."

Ron played dumb. "We are doing it." He parked his face right in front of hers. "We're almost done. Remember?" He nodded his head up and down.

Jackie wasn't amused. Her eyes flashed irritation. "I mean the presentation, to the class."

"Wha-a-at?" Was she off her rocker?

But Jackie was dead serious. Her tone was fierce. "Grandad is in the hospital dying because of those mines. I want to do it for his sake."

Ron scuffed the ground, embarrassed by the emotion in her voice.

Jackie ploughed on. "I thought that since your dad is sick too, you might want...."

Hold on now. Jackie wasn't saying that he might want to get up in front of the whole class and do that report, was she? He looked at her. That's exactly what she was saying.

Ron looked at the sky, his feet, the road, anywhere but at her. If it was anything else, he'd help her out, swear to God. But not that. Man, he couldn't get up there in front of everybody. Not for something serious like that. He couldn't. That's all there was to it.

"Never mind. Forget it." That's what her mouth said. What her eyes said was that she never really expected he would.

Ron tried to do like she said. Forget it. He should have known when he saw that look on her face in class. He could kick himself. And him thinking she had come around to his side. What a dunce he was. That's it. He was finished. He wanted nothing more to do with Jacko. He stayed away from her the rest of the day. Wasn't much trouble because she sure didn't look his way.

He was in a lousy mood all evening. At supper his mother suggested he needed to go to bed earlier and get a good night's rest. God, he hated that. Why did they automatically assume everything could be cured with a good sleep? He felt like telling her the old man didn't seem to be in much better humour after one of his sleeps.

He hung around the house. No, he wasn't going to Jackie's. Not this evening. He picked up the phone on the first ring.

"Ron?"

It was her.

"Yeah."

"Are you coming, or not?"

"Be right there."

He was out the door in such a tear he bumped right smack into his father on the way in. "What's the big rush?" his father asked.

Ron pushed past him. "Got to work on the report."

"That's the stuff."

Ron jogged in around The Bottom. Jeez, the old man was starting to act half decent. Too bad he hadn't gone to St. John's ten years ago. Ron wondered how decent he'd be if he found out Ron was going on the picket line tomorrow night. It dawned on Ron he hadn't seen a beer around the house since the old man got back. Of course it was only yesterday. Still, a record.

The Haskells' porch door was wide open. Ron stepped inside and tapped lightly on the kitchen door. Jackie called for him to come in. She had already started putting brackets around bunches of notes, using the fat pencil for some and a blue pen for others.

"Hello, Mrs. Haskell," he called to her mother in the living room.

"Hello, dear," she replied, and went on knitting and watching television.

"Here, use this one," he told Jackie, hauling the pen of many refills out of his binder. "Pick two colours."

She sized it up. "Another one! I'm gonna start calling you 'His Nibs!'"

"Ha-ha," he said.

"Whose do you want to go through first?" she asked, referring to their notes.

"Yours." As if he'd volunteer his mess.

She lowered her voice. "About what I said today. You don't have to. I shouldn't have said that. I'll do it on my own."

"No, it's okay. I'll do it." Where had that come from? He was dribbling at the mouth again.

"You will?" she said. Her face lit up.

Someone should stuff a sock down his throat. Yeah, well, he might do it, but he wasn't putting one minute of extra work into any presentation. And he might back out yet. "I s'pose," Ron's sigh was exaggerated. "You're an awful lot of trouble, you know that?"

Jackie laughed. "But some things are worth it," she said, all serious now. And she stuck her nose in her notes again.

Ron looked at Mr. Bennie's empty recliner, his mine shaft, he'd called it, its lever at rest while he lay in a hospital bed. Mr. Bennie was worth the trouble. And Jackie too. She must be. Because Ron had thought that doing the report in front of the class was the last thing in the world he wanted. But it wasn't. The last thing he wanted was to have Jackie get up there all alone.

By the time they finished going through the notes, she had her presentation all planned. Ron was still trying to decipher what he'd written.

In class the next day, Perky asked for names so she could draw up a schedule.

Ron leaned back in his seat. His leg started to jiggle. Would Jackie put up her hand?

By God, she did. Halfway anyway. "Ron and me worked with Grandad. We're doing the miners' disease and the Union...." Her voice trailed off.

Ron pretended he never saw Nicole's look.

There were a few low laughs. "Yeah, Ron. Way to go."

Ron touched his fingers to his forehead in a salute. He could handle the razzing. He hoped Jackie didn't mind too much.

As luck would have it, he came face to face with Nicole on the way out of class.

"Hi, Ron."

"Hey." He didn't know what else to say.

"Guess what?" she said. "My dad has had to go down in the mine sometimes since the strike. He told Mom they should give the men their raise. He said even with ten times the pay, he wouldn't want to work down there."

"Is that right?"

Nicole went on. "He said the men in the office want the strike to be over too. They don't like having to breathe that air underground." Looking as proud as Bert did with his inside information, she looked up at Ron. "So it might all be over soon, and everything will be back to normal."

"Normal, eh? Yeah, maybe in twenty or thirty years. That's if the mines stay closed."

"The strike won't last that long, you silly."

Nicole ran to catch her van.

Ron looked after her. She meant well. But she lived in a different world. And he knew it wasn't a world he wanted to trouble himself with.

He and Jackie worked on the report again that evening. By ten o'clock they were about three-quarters done.

"Let's finish it up this weekend," Jackie suggested. "Then we'll have some time to practise and do any fixing up we need to do."

"Sure," Ron replied. "Not tomorrow night though."

"Oh, you got big plans, have you Ron?" Her voice was flat, but she was starting to work up a bit of colour.

Ron looked straight at her. She was jealous. She was actually jealous. And doing a poor job of hiding it. "Yep," he teased, full of himself. "Been planning this a while now. Gonna get someone pretty cheesed off at me."

Jackie's eyes flashed. She snapped, "I hope you don't mean me. Because I couldn't care less what –"

He cut her off. "Take it easy! I'm talking about my old man."

"Your dad?"

He nodded. "I'm going on the picket line, with Bert."

"In the Brook? And you're not telling your dad?" She shook her head. "You're asking for trouble, Ron."

"Maybe," he said, and grinned at her on his way out the door.

FRIDAY EVENING HE WAS HOME FROM SCHOOL BY three thirty-five. He watched out the window for the Turpins' car. Bert and his father were picking him up.

There they were. Ron stuffed a slice of banana bread in his mouth and grabbed his sweater from the top of the washer. He ran around the corner of the house and yelled to his mother, who was taking clothes off the line. "Hey, Mom, I'm going with Bert. Be back around midnight."

He didn't wait for an answer. As he headed for the car, he heard her call, "Ron, come back here." He jumped in the back and pulled the door shut.

They drove out the top road and turned up towards Salt Cove Brook. It took no time at all to drive the two and a half miles to the mine site.

They cruised past the manager's big house and the road that turned off towards the rest of the Company housing. Up ahead was the main office, a long white building. There were some cars parked in front of it.

Bert's father swung to the left. He drove up to six or seven fellows standing around having a smoke in front of their vehicles. Propped up against two oil drums were Union signs with the letters CNTU. They parked next to a '67 Ford pickup.

Was this all? Not much to see.

Bert's father joined the men. Ron and Bert leaned back on the hood of the car. "This is it," Bert said importantly.

Ron nodded. He took a good look around. Directly in front, across a small brook, was a high wire-mesh fence. Behind it and up the hill loomed the mine shaft.

"There used to be twenty-five or thirty men here, but the Company got a court injunction and made them cut back."

"How come?"

Bert shrugged. "Probably afraid the men might go on a rampage or something."

"Wild."

Bert was enjoying his know-it-all status. He bobbed his head towards the fence. "That's the main gate. Company security controls that. You have to go through there to get up to the shaft. The only ones the men will let pass are the fellows who have to check on the mine, like the pumpmen or the hoist guys."

Ron nodded. "What happens if someone else tries to get through?"

Bert laughed. "Not many do. No sir. Not many do."

Ron wouldn't give Bert the satisfaction of asking him why. Bert was already too puffed up.

A couple of cars left and others took their places. The parking lot over at the office was empty now, except for one vehicle. Rick Beck was giving it dirty looks. "That's Lewin's car. I should go over there and slash —"

"Take it easy now, buddy, you're not going to slash anything." Ben Hilliar clamped a hand on Rick's shoulder. "Me and you is going to have a dandy game of cards here, after I haves a bite to eat."

Nate Edwards turned the car radio on full blast and rolled down the window. "Let's have some suppertime music."

Ron and Bert weren't too impressed with his Newfoundland jigs and reels, but they were impressed with the grub he hauled out of the back seat. Dried caplin and chocolate cupcakes. All of a sudden food was coming from everywhere. Homemade buns, a couple cans of Vienna sausages, baloney sandwiches, a tin of fruit cocktail – all laid out on the hood of Harry Slaney's Chevy Nova. It was a feast.

"Dig in, boys," said Bert's father. He tossed Bert the keys to the car. "There's some Coke in the trunk."

They sat wherever they could find a place. Bert and Ron settled themselves on an upended light pole lying on the ground. They ate and listened to the men talk, about fishing, cars, the strike, whatever came up.

Ron glanced out to the road. Two bike riders were coming around the curve. Ron recognized Nicole. She'd see him for sure. Would she wave? Should he? He hoped desperately no one would do anything...call them names, or insult them, or stuff like that. He glanced at Rick...busy eating. Ron snagged a jagged breath. Good. Keep eating, buddy.

The other person, not her sister, too old – maybe her mother – pedalled past like they weren't there. Didn't look their way at all. Nicole did though. She looked across the parking lot like she couldn't help herself. Right at Ron. Her front tire swerved, and veered towards the other bike. The other person turned and said something to her then, and she rode on.

Nicole looked back once. She waved, though she tried to make it look like she was fixing her hair. Ron waved back. He didn't bother trying to fix his hair.

After, Ron and Bert sat in the car and listened to the radio. "That was Nicole on the bike, wasn't it?"

As if Bert didn't know.

Ron fooled with the dial. "Yep."

Just as it was getting dark a truck pulled up, cruised right up tight to the security gate.

Ron was sweating. He was half afraid to look. What if it was his old man? No. It was a Chev. Saved.

A few of the boys wandered over to the truck. Bert's father followed.

"C'mon," said Bert, jumping out. "Let's see what's up."

Ron trailed after him.

When they got there it was pretty hot already. Someone had gotten out of the Chev and Rick was bent on putting the fellow back in, forcibly. Ron heard Rick say, "Listen, buddy, nobody is getting past here tonight. That goes for you and all your management friends."

Some cursing and arguing followed. Whoever was in the truck must have tried to give Rick the boots because he doubled over for a second. Then he lunged at the truck door again.

Amidst a fresh round of swearing, Rick said. "I don't care what you left in there. If you left your mudder up there the night, you wouldn't be going up to get her." Rick had a fistful of the guy's shirt.

Then Ben and Nate pulled Rick back, and Ron saw it was Vince Kearney in the truck. Vince was one of the few guys from town who were employed in management. He looked pretty sick right now, like one awful terrified guy trying not to show it.

Bert's father stepped forward. "I think you'd better get out of here, Kearney, before something happens we'll all regret."

Surrounded, Kearney didn't have much choice. Red-faced and angry, he slid back behind the wheel. He was no longer neatly tucked in, and a jacket button was missing.

Rick wrestled free from Nate. He made another grab for the door and leaned in to Kearney's face. "Don't plan on stopping by the club anytime soon. You might come out to find your car over the causeway." His laugh was harsh. "Bad brakes."

Ron let out a long breath and sat down on the light pole. This was wicked stuff. He kind of felt sorry for Kearney.

Bert sat next to him. "Enough action for you, Tarrant?"

The words weren't out of his mouth when another set of lights came over the hill. The men poured tea from their thermoses and didn't pay much attention. Bert looked at Ron. "What now?"

The lights came closer. Ron knew. He'd been waiting for it. His stomach churned. He shouldn't have eaten. He should have waited.

"It's a pickup," said Bert.

Ron could see that.

"Jeez, Ron, I think it's your old man."

Ron could see that too. Now if he could just breathe.

He'd been half expecting this. Been pushing it to the back of his mind. The dread had been there though, all evening. Except now it was all over him, and inside, in his bones and his blood.

The pickup swerved across the parking lot at the old man's usual maniac speed. If that didn't get everyone's attention, the headlights mowing them down sure did. There was a screech of brakes. Before the truck came to a complete stop, the old man was out, lights flaring, door hanging wide.

Ron steeled himself for the worst.

No one moved.

Ron stood up, his breath shallow. He felt more in control on his feet. His fists clenched at his sides. His insides shrank together, tough and tight.

The old man barged towards him, like some raving lunatic. He jerked his thumb towards the cab. "Get your carcass in that truck."

Ron planted his feet good and solid. He'd known all along the St. John's niceties couldn't last. It wasn't in the old man's nature. Ron was mortified. Too ashamed to be afraid. What would the old man pull in front of Bert and everybody?

"I'm staying till the shift's over," Ron said, low and stubborn. He was surprised at his calm. What was his father going to do, beat him up right here?

Bert's father stepped in then. "How you doing, Leo? Is there a problem?"

The old man dropped back a step. His arm fell stiff to his side. "Yeah, there's a problem," he growled. "He got no business being here."

Ron shook his head. Man, what an embarrassment.

"Well now, that depends," said Bert's father. "I've been bringing my young fella all along. I thinks it's good for them to see what's going on." He paused. Took a drag on his cigarette. "In the meantime, I wouldn't have let Ron come if I'd known...."

The old man did up his jacket. He wheezed and coughed. Glanced around him. Looked flustered. He nodded to Ben and Nate. Seemed to simmer down. "No harm done, I guess," he muttered.

Bert's father gave a short knowing laugh. "Look at it this way. At least you know where he is."

A grunt in response.

He walked Ron's dad back to the truck. They stood and talked for a while. Ron couldn't hear what they were saying. He didn't want to.

As the truck pulled away, Bert's father called, "I'll drop him off around midnight."

Ron didn't hear his father's reply. Didn't want to.

After he'd gone though, and Ron had met up with his breath again, he couldn't help but think about his old man. He was different. A week ago he would have hauled Ron out of here no matter what anyone said. And the change had to do with his trip to St. John's.

Once more fear put the squeeze on Ron's breath.

Not fear of the old man this time – but fear for him.

14

THERE WAS NO FIST IN THE WINDOW WHEN Ron got home. And nothing about the picket line the next day. In fact, the whole weekend went by without Friday night being mentioned at all, by anyone. Ron didn't know if he was more grateful or disappointed.

The unspoken words saturated the air though, threatening to blow up into a good row any minute. When Bert phoned, the old man gave Ron a dirty look.

"Now, Leo," said Ron's mother, manoeuvring the broom under the table.

Ron's father glared while Ron talked with Bert.

Ron deliberately took his time. He grinned as he hung up. "Relax, Dad! He just wanted to know if there's a game this evening."

Another glare before the old man went back to reading the television guide.

Ron's mother said, "You stop your aggravating.

You done enough this weekend." Even when she was mad, she couldn't look mean. "Don't you have some homework?"

"It's only Saturday, Mom. And I'm going to Jackie's to finish up the report. You should be proud of me, working on a Saturday night!"

An exasperated look from his mother. Ron wondered how much his father had told her last night. She'd probably kept the old man's fist out of the window, and out of Ron's face.

He gave his mother a peck on the cheek and was out the door before she could ask when he'd be home.

JACKIE WASTED NO TIME IN GETTING THEM BOTH to work. "I went to see Grandad this afternoon," she informed Ron. "I told him we finished the report. He wants us to go see him and read it to him."

"You told him we were done? We're not —"

"Well, I am. I finished mine last night. So, all we have to do is read through yours and fix up a few mistakes."

"More than a few, I'd say."

"Can't be that much." Jackie reached for his notes. "Here, let me see."

Ron wanted to shove them under the table.

Hide them from her any way he could. Instead, he gripped the pages in both hands and inched them across the table to her.

Jackie laughed and tugged them away from him. She started to read. Ron was sweating. And Jacko wasn't helping. She squinted and peered at some line or other. She turned the page and looked puzzled for a paragraph or two, and raised her eyebrows at another part. She finished and looked at him. "Not bad, Tarrant."

"Sure, I didn't need you to tell me that." Ron was so puffed up the buttons on his shirt would have popped if there'd been any. And his face, slack-jawed and smiling, was making a proper fool of him.

Jackie picked up her pen. "There's a few things here." She found the line she was looking for and said, "You need a period and a capital there. And you have *ventilation* spelled wrong."

Ron sighed painfully loud, and glowered at her.

She laughed. "I don't want you to get too full of yourself."

"Some chance of that."

Jackie decided they should alternate their presentations, with her addressing the working conditions and health issues and Ron dealing with the growth of the Union and the strikes. Ron just wanted to get done. After they'd decided on the order of things, they practised reading it aloud. Ron was impressed. It sounded pretty good. He didn't know about going to the hospital and reading it though.

"How about if I just give Mr. Bennie my copy to read when he feels like it? He mightn't feel up to listening to all this."

"You don't know Grandad very well. He's been asking when we're going to be done." Jackie looked at Ron. "You don't want to do it, do you?"

"No, it's not that." Ron didn't bat an eye at his lie.

"Well, I'm reading mine. You can do what you like." Jackie flicked her hair off her forehead and stood up, her report in her hand.

Man, this Jacko was stubborn. Ron made a show of hastily shuffling his papers. "You needn't think you're going to sneak off without me and get all the credit for yourself."

Jackie laughed. "You really are cracked, did I ever tell you that?" She pulled the door closed behind them.

"You're gonna miss me, Jacko, when we're all finished with this report, if we ever are."

She shot him an incredulous look. "Me? Miss you?"

Then she laughed. "I'll miss you all right. Like a boil."

Ron laughed too, but with relief. For a minute

there he'd thought she was serious. "Of course, if you ever need me to help you again...."

He dodged Jackie's shove.

They bantered back and forth until they reached the hospital road. Then the conversation turned serious. "Grandad's in a private room," Jackie said. "There might be some relatives there, besides Mom." Her tone prepared him.

"How's he doing?"

She didn't answer right away. She shifted her papers to the other arm. "Not too good. He can't sleep unless he's propped up with about a dozen pillows. That's the only way he can breathe. And he can't keep anything down."

They walked in silence.

"He used to play soccer, you know. Centre forward. Mom said he was really good. He was known all over the Peninsula."

"That's why he always asked if there was a game before he set up a time to talk to us."

Jackie nodded.

They reached the hospital steps and went in. Ron had never been in this part, where the patients were. He followed Jackie down the hall to her grandfather's room.

Mrs. Haskell was there, sitting on one side of the bed. On the other side was a couple Ron didn't know, probably from up the shore.

Mrs. Haskell motioned for them to come in. Jackie stood at the foot of the bed. "Hi, Aunt Gert, Uncle Dave," she said when she got a chance to get a word in. Ron edged inside the door and leaned against the wall. He nodded to Aunt Gert and Uncle Dave when Jackie's mom introduced him.

Pillowed up in bed with the hospital gown on, Mr. Bennie looked twice as old as he had sitting in his green recliner at home. Twice as thin, twice as sick. His eyes stayed closed.

Jackie's mother got up and laid her hand on his forehead.

Mr. Bennie stirred and moaned.

"Dad," she said quietly, "Jackie and Ron are here."

Mr. Bennie moved. His eyes fluttered under his lids.

"Do you feel up to hearing their report?"

He opened his eyes and stared, unfocused. Then, struggling to pull himself up higher on the pillows, he broke out in a coughing fit. Immediately they were all up around him, holding him, fluffing pillows behind his back. The coughing went on and on, a long-drawn-out spell that left Mr. Bennie gasping for breath.

Ron couldn't take it. He stepped out in the hallway.

He searched up and down the short corridor.

Where were the bloody nurses? Couldn't they hear what was going on? Rita Byrne came on the run then and went into the room. He heard her calm voice. She stayed until the coughing subsided.

By the time Ron slipped back inside, Rita was straightening the sheets and holding a water glass and straw to Mr. Bennie's lips.

"Thank you, dear," Mr. Bennie said hoarsely. He patted her hand. "Sorry to bother you."

"Don't you worry about bothering me. Sure, that's what I'm here for." She straightened up. Her friendly loud voice seemed out of place in this cramped sick room. "I'll be back in a while to check on you."

After she left, Mr. Bennie seemed to rest easier.

The adults chatted intermittently across the bed.

Jackie laid a hand on her grandfather's arm. "Grandad, would you like Ron and me to read our report?"

Her grandfather smiled weakly at her, and covered her hand with his.

Ron looked at them. He kind of felt left out.

"We can do it another time if you want."

Mr. Bennie shook his head. "You tell that young skipper to come closer." He breathed heavily. "So I can hear what ye've got to say."

Jackie beckoned. "C'mon, Ron. Here's your chance to show off."

Show off. All Ron wanted to do was take off.

Mrs. Haskell motioned for Ron to come closer. But Uncle Dave had hopped to his feet and given his wife a good poke in the arm. "No need for that, Marion," he said to Jackie's mother. "Gert and I will stretch our legs a bit and the youngsters can sit here in our chairs."

"Certainly," said Aunt Gert, and used Uncle Dave's arm to prise herself to her feet.

While Jackie was reading, Ron stole a look at Mr. Bennie. Why would he want to hear this, sick like he was? But Jackie's grandad wasn't brooding. He was intent on Jackie's words. He nodded as he listened. Once he corrected a date.

Ron's turn. His cold hands clutched the paper. "The St. Lawrence Workers Protective Union played an important role in the lives of the miners." He was nervous. He could hear it in his voice.

Mr. Bennie nodded encouragement as he had with Jackie, till Ron forgot his nerves and concentrated on getting it right. He did too. He knew when he finished. Mr. Bennie looked at Jackie and him and held out a hand to each of them. He never said a word, just squeezed their hands tight and nodded, over and over.

Ron never saw Mr. Bennie alive again.

JACKIE WASN'T IN SCHOOL THURSDAY MORNING. Sister Pat told them at the start of class that her grandfather had died during the night.

Ron's head dropped to his desk. He squeezed his eyes shut to block everything out, but it only made the images in his mind sharper. Mr. Bennie in his recliner. Mr. Bennie telling his stories, battling for every breath. His little jokes. His wink at Ron when they'd teased Jackie. His eyes brimming with tears when Ron and Jackie had read their report for him in the hospital.

Ron hung around till recess. Then he snuck out. He walked out the school road towards the cemetery. There must have been a half-dozen cars parked in front of the Haskells' house. All they needed was him hanging around.

HE WENT BACK THAT EVENING. PRETENDED HE was walking past. No sign of Jackie. Still lots of cars. He walked up as far as the old soccer field and turned back. He should go up to the door. Not like he hadn't been at the Haskells' before. Maybe he'd go home and phone. He was past the house, about to turn the corner by the substation. He looked back. If she'd only come out.

Enough of this. He turned around, braced himself, and walked back to the house. He knocked and waited on the step.

Jackie opened the door.

A shaky sigh of relief from Ron. "Hi. I..." he began.

"Hi..." Jackie started at the same time.

They both shut up. There was an awkward silence.

"I'll come out," she said, glancing behind her. "It's pretty crowded in the house."

They sat on the steps.

Ron started again. "I'm sorry about your grandad."

"Thanks," said Jackie. That was all.

Ron wasn't sure what to do. Was it okay to stay for a while? He wanted to. And he didn't feel Jackie wanted to be rid of him. He sensed that she was glad he had come by. But he didn't know what to say to her either. So he just sat there on the step with her and let her be. He did get up once to get her jacket from the porch and put it around her shoulders.

Finally Jackie spoke. "Grandad really likes – really liked you, you know."

Ron picked a thread off his cuff and twisted it around his finger. He fumbled for the right words. "I liked him too. He sure knows...knew...a lot of stuff."

People were arriving for the wake. They were

having to move aside every few minutes to let someone in or out of the house. Ron stood up to let Aunt Milly Shea, who was as wide as the step, go by. "I'd better be off," he said.

"Do you want to come in and see Grandad first?"

Ron nodded. "Okay."

He didn't really. He would rather remember Mr. Bennie sitting in his recliner, his shaft he called it, telling him and Jackie a yarn.

But he wanted to be respectful. And the last thing he wanted right now was to hurt Jackie. If she wanted him to see her grandad, that's what he'd do. So he followed Jackie inside through the people crowding the kitchen and into the front room where Mr. Bennie was being waked. He walked with Jackie to the casket.

Mr. Bennie was laid out in a black suit and white shirt, black rosary beads draped around his white hands, folded across his chest like he was having a peaceful rest. All his fights were over. For the miners. For life. For every breath.

Ron bowed his head. How long was he supposed to stay?

His mind was emptier than it was for a history test. And his feelings were numb. He figured he should feel something more when it was Mr. Bennie lying here.

He couldn't feel sadness, or regret, or anything until he turned around and saw Gord Murphy, that lazy tub of lard, who never put in a good day's work in his life, lying back in Mr. Bennie's recliner as if he owned it. And then he felt anger.

The gall of that fellow. It wasn't right for someone like that to be settled back in Mr. Bennie's armchair.

Ron's head pounded. Gord Murphy was getting out of that chair. That much was certain.

In the room, besides himself and Jackie, there was only Gord and old Mr. Clarke, leaning on his cane by the casket.

Ron walked up to Gord. When he smelled Gord's beer breath, his insides heaved in a swell of disgust. "This is Mr. Bennie's chair," he said in Gord's ear. "If you had any respect you'd stay out of it."

Ron straightened up fast. Mrs. Haskell had come into the room with some people.

Gord stayed right where he was.

Ron was the one who left. He flicked his hand to tell Jackie he was leaving and tore out of the house before he went savage on Gord Murphy.

15

PERKY WAS NO SLOUCH WHEN IT CAME TO correcting. By Tuesday she had the reports done and wasted no time in passing them back. That was decent at least. Most teachers droned on and on before passing anything back, figured it was their job to get you good and depressed before delivering the final blow.

Not that Ron had ever gotten even mildly despondent over any kind of test or assignment. A below-fifty mark just meant he had to do marginally better the next time, and anything above fifty meant he could take it easy for a while.

He sprawled in his desk as Perky walked up and down the rows. He knew he was okay with this one. It was good for a C, at least. Perky delivered the report right into his hand. A big fat B! Surpassed himself, he had. Ron couldn't remember ever getting a B since leaving elementary school. Not bad, Tarrant. Not bad at all. He'd have to leave this one lying around the house. It had to be worth something. Even the old man couldn't scoff this time.

Rubbernecks craned to get a look. Ron flashed his B. Give them a treat.

Nicole grinned at him across the room. "I beat you," she mouthed playfully, showing her A.

Ron mouthed back. "Teacher's pet."

"Sore loser," Nicole returned.

Then Perky was at Ron's desk again. "Ron, will you return Jackie's paper to her? I'm sure she'd like to see it before she comes back."

Ron nodded. He was going to the funeral this afternoon. He hadn't told or asked anyone, but he was. He wouldn't give it to her there though. Some other time. He glanced down at Jackie's paper. An A+ she got. She deserved it.

The funeral service was two o'clock. Ron killed an hour after lunch at Harry's playing pinball. By the time he left there the fog, thick as pea soup all morning, had turned into a steady drizzle. Ron didn't mind that so much, but then before he got halfway up the harbour the sky opened up. What a downpour! And him right in the middle of it. He mouthed some choice words and took off at a run. Drops fat as grubs soaked him front and back, and he arrived at the church drenched to the skin. No wonder there wasn't a single smoker hanging around the door. Ron scuttled inside too.

The place was packed. Mass had already begun. Shivering in his sodden clothes, Ron slid into the last pew and slicked back his hair with a damp hand. The waves were pretty flat now.

He could see the casket in the aisle at the front. He couldn't make out Jackie in the rows of black mourning clothes. While Ron was still searching the crowd he felt a nudge at his elbow. He looked up and standing there was his father, nudging him again.

Ron was stunned. And he must have looked it because the old man gave him a harder push. "Move in," he growled, and edged into the pew.

Ron, dazed as he was, shuffled over to make room. Himself, right here in the pew. Mr. Bennie had done what Ron's mother hadn't been able to do – get the old man inside the church.

But why park himself right here? Probably to nail Ron after about skipping. Ron didn't care. It just meant another bawling out when he got home. He was used to that.

Father Delaney droned on in a litany of praying. All Ron could take in was his old man next to him, knees cracking as he folded himself up on the kneeler, flicking his hand in the sign of the cross. And the breath, loud and laboured as though drawing air through a clogged filter.

Ron found himself minding his father's breathing more than he was the priest. In the quiet around them he was aware of every noisy intake of air. Every now and then he'd sneak a sideways glance at his father, trying to gauge how he was. How come he hadn't noticed his father's breathing before? Mom must know. She hadn't said a word about it.

He craned his neck to find her up front in her usual spot. Today she was farther back because the funeral procession took up most of the front section. He'd liked to have been able to go up and ask her right away, but it would have to wait until later.

Ron did manage to listen when Father talked about Mr. Bennie's contributions to the Union and to the town. Ron hadn't known the half of it. By the time Father was finished, there were wet eyes and sniffles all through the church. Ron wished Father would get on with it before his own watery eyes leaked over.

He couldn't say for sure if his dad was affected too, but the coarse breathing got heavier and louder until it was a harsh rattle in his father's chest. In no time it worked up to a relentless hacking that left him so worn out he had to sit for a spell while everyone stood for a hymn.

Ron's anxious glance took in his father's perspiring forehead. He didn't even have a tissue to give him. All through the singing Ron kept turning to see how his dad was doing. Finally, he stood with everyone else. Ron breathed easier.

Father Delaney said the final solemn blessing. The congregation remained standing while the casket was wheeled out of the church by the pallbearers, all miners in their Sunday best. The family followed. It was hard to watch. Hard to think Mr. Bennie wouldn't be there in his chair when Ron went to give Jackie her A+ report. And it was harder still when he saw Jackie, staring straight ahead, her yellow jacket the only bit of colour amidst the mourners. He should have told her he was coming to the mass. She wouldn't see him way over here.

Hey, he wasn't the only one skipping school. Donna popped out of a pew as Jackie passed by, linked her arm through Jackie's, and walked with her. Not only that. Sister Pat was in the same pew along with a couple more girls.

Well, the old man couldn't say much to Ron when even the nuns were skipping out for the funeral. And taking half the school with them.

Everyone started to file out. Ron waited for his father to move. Finally the old man released his grip on the pew in front of them and straightened up. "Tell your mother I'll be in the truck."

Ron began to make his way towards his mother. And Sister Pat made her way towards him. Oh, oh. Now he would catch it.

"Hello, Ron," she said softly. "I'm glad you're here. You were privileged to know Mr. Bennie."

Ron found himself filling up. He couldn't talk. It was that word *privileged.* She was right. He pulled himself together and nodded. "I was," he said.

And he meant it.

Sister squeezed his elbow and let him pass.

Ron moved on. He cleared his throat. Sister Pat was all right.

They drove home mostly in silence, except for the squeaky windshield wipers and his mother's comments on the lovely service and what a terrible day it was for a funeral. Any day would be terrible for a funeral, Ron figured, but he kept his thoughts to himself. It seemed to him it should be this kind of day, especially for a man like Mr. Bennie. There was thunder and lightning when Jesus died, wasn't there? If the religion classes were telling the truth, he had been a good man too.

Ron moved to open the truck door.

"I'm going to the graveyard," his father said, shoving the gearstick into reverse. "You can come if you like."

"Okay," Ron said, letting his mother out. They exchanged glances. Her look warned him not to start anything.

"Leo," she said, frowning with worry, "do you

think you should be out in weather like this?"

Leo ignored her. They roared out of the yard.

There weren't many people at the cemetery. The weather was just too bloody miserable. The family had already gathered at the gravesite. Jackie was there. She sure looked sad, on the end, kind of by herself. Ron was glad when Alice, the older sister, put an arm around her.

The wind had come up, driving sheets of rain right in their faces. Father Delaney said a brief graveside prayer. Then, at his urging, the family agreed to return home. But not until the casket was lowered. As they walked down the hill the men began to fill in the grave.

Ron's father grabbed a shovel and dug into the pile of dirt at the gravesite. After a few turns he was winded, and leaned heavily on the handle.

Ron slogged through the muck to him. "Here, Dad," he said, taking the shovel, "I'll finish it."

In no time the grave was filled in. Ves Tobin collected the mud-caked shovels and tossed them in the back of his pickup. One by one the men bowed heads and touched the temporary wooden cross before leaving the gravesite.

Ron's father lingered, his hand still on the white marker. He rubbed at the muddy finger-prints left by the men but couldn't clean the grimy smudges any more than he could wipe the yellow tobacco stains from his own fingers.

Ron talked around the lump in his throat. "C'mon, Dad, you're soaked." Without a word they walked down the hill.

On the drive out the cemetery road to the pavement, Ron sat, his arm along the seat back, looking at his father. He drove hunched over the wheel. Oblivious to the wet hair plastered to his scalp and wet clothes to his skin, his mind was off somewhere. Probably still at the gravesite.

Ron wanted to bring him back to the here and now. "Mr. Bennie told me you were a good miner."

His father's response was to jack up the heat and turn on the fan full blast.

Ron raised his voice over the fan. "One of the best, he said."

His father reached in his shirt pocket for a cigarette. Distracted, he let the pack slide back. He didn't say anything.

Ron was glad he'd told him anyway.

They were driving around the Riverhead bend before his father spoke. "He was a good man. He treated everyone the same. If you needed a hand he pitched in, not like some of them."

At home Ron changed into dry clothes before rummaging for something to eat. His report still sat on the table where he'd tossed it at noon. Mom would have read it. But not Dad. Not likely.

Mom set the teapot on the back of the stove. "Ron, that's a good job you did with that report." She looked at her husband. "Isn't that right, Leo?"

Leo, in the middle of a sip of tea, grunted.

Ron turned away. He figured his efforts were worth more than a grunt. But he couldn't get worked up right now. He didn't even want to. Didn't have the energy for it. If his father wasn't interested, then that's just the way it was. Maybe he had other things on his mind, bigger than a piddling research paper. Things like his job. Or his life.

Dad set the mug down. "Yes, this is a good paper," he said, picking up the report. "A darn fine one, I'd say."

Ron choked on his jam-jam cookie. He swallowed hard and ran himself a drink of water. Was he hearing right? A big, sloppy grin snuck across his face.

He watched his father leaf through the pages. "I hardly believed you did it till your mother convinced me." He looked at Ron, a normal look, with not a trace of criticism. "And if you can do it once, you can do it all the time."

Ron helped himself to another handful of jam-jams. He groaned aloud. What had he gotten himself into? Now his father was going too far. A slight bit of interest would do. No need to go overboard with it.

"Dad," he said, choosing his words carefully. "This time was different. Mr. Bennie gave me a lot of help." He paused. "But he's not here anymore." He hoped Mr. Bennie would forgive him, would understand what was at stake.

The old man snorted and looked at his wife. "No. But his granddaughter is. Seems to me you weren't hightailing it in The Bottom every evening after supper just to see Mr. Bennie."

Ron was speechless. And red. Because it was true. He did like Jackie. But he didn't like the fact that his parents, Dad especially, knew about it. Now he supposed they'd be watching his every move and commenting on it. What a pain.

They sat there chuckling at him, the two of them. What could he say? Let them have their little laugh. Glad he could be of service.

He looked out the window so they couldn't see his face.

The rain had let up. Wayne, using his school bag and jacket for goalposts, kicked ball in front of the house. By the look of him he'd been playing in the rain too.

Ron thought this was as good a time as any to have a few kicks with Wayne.

His brother was delighted and jumped around like a yappy little mutt. When Ron let him get a goal, Wayne just about turned himself inside out.

SISTER PAT GAVE JACKIE THE BETTER PART OF A week before she asked if they were ready to do their report. In fact, Jackie and Ron were the last ones.

"I don't know if I can do it," Jackie told him between classes.

"Sure you can," Ron reassured her, tweaking a strand of hair that fell over her face. Funny how things had turned around. Now he was the one trying to convince Jackie she could do it.

"What if I start to cry up there in front of the whole class?"

"I'll just take over and do my part. No one will even notice."

He knew he had to get her through this. Get them both through it.

They stood at the front of the room. After a few shaky breaths, everything went fine. The class was listening. The whole class. Really listening. Their voices grew steadier and stronger with each turn.

They were nearing the end. Ron read his last part, outlining the strike issues, like the right of workers to refuse to work in unsafe areas. As he read, Jackie, in the background, began to roll call the names of deceased miners.

Then it was Jackie's final turn. She highlighted some of the conclusions from the report of the Royal Commission. Ron took over and called the names. As she finished he read the final name, "Mr. Bennie Lake."

There was silence. Then some sniffles and nose blowing. Ron and Jackie walked back to their seats. No one stirred to leave, though the sounds of dismissal could be heard in the corridor. Sister Pat stood in front, hands folded. "Thank you, Jackie. Thank you, Ron. From all of us." She paused. "Class is dismissed."

They were a subdued lot filing out. Ron waited for Jackie to gather her things. There were a few stragglers, one of them Nicole. She hesitated, clutched her binder in front of her like a shield, and walked over to Jackie. "I'm sorry about your grandfather – and everything," she said. Jackie nodded and murmured thanks.

Nicole walked up the row. "Good job, Ron," she said. Her voice was sad and so was the half smile she mustered up.

He nodded. "Thanks. You too." She was nice all right, almost as nice as Jackie.

Ron and Jackie walked out of the school together, down Church Lane and past the post office.

Busy there today. Mail must have gotten in late. There were cars and people all over the place.

Ron felt a none-too-gentle punch in the arm. He turned.

"How ya doing, Tarrant?" said Mick-Joe, giving his crazy loon laugh. He squeezed Ron's shoulder hard. Ron endured it.

"Not bad." No telling what Mick-Joe would say or do.

Mick-Joe, a St. Pierre cigarillo stuck in his mouth, eyed Jackie. "Now, Tarrant," he said, eyes half closed against the smoke, "that's more like it." He hooted again and turned up to the post office, calling back over his shoulder. "At least you're on the right side now."

Yeah, but not for Mick-Joe's reasons. "What's it to you?" he yelled at Mick-Joe's back.

Jackie looked from Mick-Joe to Ron. "What's that all about?"

"Nothing." Ron said.

"I don't believe you, Ron." She swung her book bag at his legs. "You're not leaving till you tell me."

"How about if we go for a walk after supper? We'll talk about it." He grinned at her.

"All right. And you better tell me." She made a face at him and took the road that went in around The Bottom.

Ron grinned and waved. He turned down the harbour.

B ETTY FITZPATRICK DORION is the author of two previous Coteau juvenile fiction titles: *Bay Girl* won the Children's Literature Award at the Saskatchewan Book Awards and was a finalist for the Publishing in Education Award in the same competition; *Melanie Bluelake's Dream* was a finalist for the Silver Birch Award in Ontario, the Young Readers' Choice Award in Manitoba and for two Saskatchewan Book Awards as well.

Born and raised in Newfoundland, Betty Dorion moved to Saskatchewan in 1975. She continues writing and teaching in that province, in Prince Albert.